THE TRAIN
AND
THE SECRET WITNESS

MIKE IKE CHINWUBA

To order additional copies of this book, contact:
Xlibris
800-056-3182
www.Xlibrispublishing.co.uk
Orders@Xlibrispublishing.co.uk
731886

CONTENTS

Chapter 1 1

Chapter 2 9

Chapter 3 13

Chapter 4 19

Chapter 5 27

Chapter 6 33

Chapter 7 41

Chapter 8 47

Chapter 9 55

Chapter 10 63

Chapter 11 71

Chapter 12 75

Chapter 13 83

Chapter 14 93

Chapter 15 97

Chapter 16 103

Chapter 17 111

Chapter 18 117

Chapter 19 121

Chapter 20 129

Chapter 21 135

Chapter 22 139

Chapter 23 143

Chapter 24 147

Chapter 25 151

Chapter 26 155

Roger was in reminiscent of the days gone-by when he was some sort of a tramp aimlessly gallivanting from station to station without any particular destination. Deep down, he cherished all the antics and shenanigans that were always taking place within the grand theatre of the train carriages by total strangers, a stage on which it was free for all to perform irrespective of talent. It was a natural mandate by which the song in every-one's heart filtered out and inevitably escaped uncontrollably like the smoke from the tiniest of seams.

=======================================

==

Dare to believe in that song in your heart
Dare to believe in the dreams
You'll dance as long as you dare to believe

==

Buddhism teaches that all problems, difficulties or
challenges can be transformed into value creation.

==

Good fortune does not lie far away.
Our lives themselves are entities of good fortune,
entities of happiness as indestructible as diamond.
_by Daisaku Ikeda

==

CHAPTER 1

Victoria station was littered with the British transport police standing in groups at each of the ticket barriers on that summer's day. The station was very busy as usual with passengers hurriedly entering and exiting or simply on transit to catch another train to their destinations as it served as a central London railway terminus and London Underground complex - making it a very busy hub for many train stations and tubes, as such; there was never a dull moment in Victoria station.

It was during the morning rush-hour on that eventful day that a train arrived and slowly hurtled on to one of the platforms and stopped, passengers started to alight and were making their way towards the ticket barrier to exit. Suddenly, a young man was seen clutching a briefcase as he struggled to power through a long queue of passengers, pushing and shoving and rapidly making his way to the ticket barrier. On reaching the ticket barrier, he had no alternative but to jump over it, as he had no ticket to let himself through and before one of the transport police officers could stop him, he launched the briefcase in front of them and disappeared into the crowd. There was total pandemonium, the groups of the transport police officers abruptly dispersed in fear, wondering if the content was ominous. The briefcase laid on the floor and no-one was seen within twenty metres of it.

Within minutes the police swarmed the station including fire fighters and several fire engines. The police were busy talking into their communication devices and trying to prevent passengers who were arriving or departing getting closer to the briefcase. In no time at-all, the area was cordoned and most of the ticket barriers closed. About three police dogs were seen milling around, attempting to unleash themselves from their handlers as they sniffed around frantically. About an hour later, a robot was despatched to apparently diffuse the content of the brief-case in case it was an explosive device. The crowd were in total grip of anxiety and fear as they awaited for the eventual detonation of the brief-case with the aid of the robot.

As the robot began to move towards the briefcase, the anxiety and fear turned into excitement and fascination as they held their breath. The robot reached the brief-case, encircled it, poked at it but there was no reaction which supposedly meant there was no explosive device detected in the briefcase. This time sigh of relief could almost be heard from the crowd. So, the robot retreated to base which was about thirty metres away to where a military personnel by the name of Jason, was operating the remote control which enabled the robot stood still, he meticulously checked the robot's data and conferred with the police inspector Collin Smith, who was in charge of the operation.

"Data suggest there is no explosive device in the brief-case", said the military personnel.

"Not good enough, I want the damn thing blown up before I send any of my men near it, that's the only way to be sure," replied Inspector Colin Smith.

"Okay, that's pretty easy," said Jason, "I like blowing things up."

He quickly reprogrammed the robot and sent it on its way back to the briefcase. With a smile he said to Inspector Smith, "Watch the stuff go boom!"

"Yeah, let's do it," said Inspector Smith, he stood aside and watched.

The Robot set off again towards the briefcase, this time slowly but steadily. When it reached it, it placed a device on it and returned quickly to Jason who was operating it.

Then the brief-case exploded with a loud cacophony of sound - 'boom!' and the crowd who had been watching with anxiety took cover while some of them turned away and ran for their lives. As a result of the explosion, fifty pound notes rained down on the terminal littering the entire area while some of the notes were still airborne. Everyone was dumbfounded when it was realized that the cash was indeed the contents of the brief-case. The crowd instantly drifted closer and closer to descend on the fifty pound notes but were restrained by the team of police officers.

"Wow! I have never blown up bundles of cash before," said Jason with his jaws dropped.

"Loads of money here, how come? Asked Inspector Collin Smith.

"Don't ask me, I have no idea" replied Jason.

"What do you make of it? The Inspector asked.

"What do you mean? Asked Jason.

"The reason behind hurling it at the police and running away," said the Inspector.

"Do you mean why he did not run away with the money?" asked Jason.

"Yes, that's the point, 'why?" the Inspector asked.

"When you find out, please do let us know – Inspector," said Jason

"You bet," replied the Inspector.

The Inspector, was pacing to and fro while his men were swiftly collecting the fifty pound notes which almost took the rest of the day to complete because some of the notes were found inside the nooks and crannies of the station including on the train-tracks. After a few weeks of deliberation, the total amount of money successfully retrieved was confirmed as three hundred thousand pounds, all in fifty pound notes.

The result of the CCTV examinations that followed identified the young man who launched the brief-case as the nineteen-year-old Roger Dean. He was from a middle class family and both his parents were politicians who had walked the corridors of power for almost two decades. With this new development, Inspector Colin Smith in no time at-all proceeded to his parents' home in order to find him and to find out where and how he got all that money and why he had to dispose of them the way he did. It was early in the morning that the Inspector arrived at Roger's parents' address. Mr Dean, Roger's father, opened the door to the Inspector who immediately showed him his ID and asked Mr Dean if Roger was available:

"Roger? Enquired Mr Dean.

"Yes, we believe he is your son, said the Inspector.

Mr Dean then opened the door wider and asked him to come in. As the Inspector stepped inside, Mr Dean closed the door and proceeded towards the dining room while the Inspector followed right behind him. In the dining room, the table was adorned with breakfast cereal, pot of tea, and some broadsheet newspapers such as, 'Daily telegraph' and The Times Newspaper. Marie, Roger's mother, was seated at one end of the table, cup of tea in one hand, immersed herself between the pages of the newspaper which laid open on the table, she was nonchalant to the Inspector's presence.

"Marie, the police Inspector is here," said Mr Dean.

Marie gradually lifted her head from the newspaper she was engrossed in and with astonishment,

"Police inspector? She asked as she peered through her reading glasses.

"Yes, he is looking for Roger," said Mr Dean

"Well, he has come to the wrong place then," said Marie.

"Please sit down Inspector," requested Mr Dean.

As the Inspector sat down, he removed a picture from his top pocket and showed it to both of them to which they confirmed he was their son - Roger.

"What has happened to him? Enquired Marie.

"Is he alright? Asked Mr Dean.

"We will like to ask him some questions," replied the Inspector.

"He does not live here anymore," said Mr Dean.

"Last time we saw Roger was about eight months ago," said Marie.

"Do you know where he might be? The Inspector asked

"We have not the foggiest idea," replied Marie.

Mr Dean poured himself a cup of tea and offered one to the Inspector to which he declined, he informed the Inspector that Roger was their only child and that he sent him to a very good boarding school where he seemed to be doing very well. He was a happy chap and was popular amongst his friends. Mr Dean expressed that he and his wife, Marie, were quite pleased at Roger's extra-ordinary progress with his studies to become a Lawyer despite his strong objection to go to university. Mr Dean confirmed that Roger eventually but reluctantly changed his mind and went to study law due to the power of his persuasion.

In the summer of the previous year, Roger's life took a turn for the worse, his world rapidly turned upside down taking his parents' world with it as well. Roger came home for the summer holidays and was getting ready to travel to South America with some of his friends from the same university. Roger and his friends had organised a party before their scheduled departure. At the party, something happened that profoundly changed his personality. When he came home very early the following morning, he slept all day. The following morning, he was still in his bedroom and did not join his parents for breakfast. So, his mother, very much concerned, swiftly went to his room and found him unconscious in bed, she quickly called an ambulance which took him to the hospital.

The doctor could not find anything wrong with him but suggested that perhaps his drink had been tampered with at the party. Since then he would stay in his room and would not make any contact with his parents or anyone. He stayed in his room for days without food or bath. After a few days that followed, his parents went into his room to check if he needed to be taken to the hospital again for another check-up. When they entered his room, to their horror, he was not there, he was gone and they had not seen him since the last eight months. Occasionally he would drop a line to his parents that he was okay but no address or phone number to which he would be traced. The contents of his room were intact, he had not taken anything with him.

The Inspector listened with great concentration to the story about Roger. He was wondering why a clever young man from a good family had turned out that way. He was unknown to the police,

"Has he ever been involved with drugs? Asked the Inspector

"Drugs? Mr Dean retorted

"Yes, drugs", repeated the Inspector

"Roger is not the type to meddle with drugs, how dare you," Marie furiously replied.

"He was found with a lot of money at Victoria station," said the Inspector.

"A lot of money, drugs, what are you on about Inspector? Asked Mr Dean defiantly.

"Roger had a briefcase containing more than three hundred thousand pounds, so the question remains – how or where he got it from," said the Inspector,

"We have no idea where he is, according to information received, he scaled a ticket barrier, launched a briefcase at the police and disappeared into the crowd," the Inspector added.

At this point there was stunning silence for a good couple of minutes, the inspector turned around and walked to the front door, with slight hesitation removed a card from his top pocket and walked back to the dining room where Mr Dean and Marie were still seating in silence staring into nothingness. The Inspector left the card containing his telephone number on the table:

"Please do give me a call if you hear from him, I will keep in touch". Said the Inspector

He walked back to the front door and left swiftly.

CHAPTER 2

Roger was on the train, the southwest train was heading to Richmond, a small but affluent suburb of Surrey which is just outside London. As usual, he was glancing through a free local newspaper, intermittently peering over the top of the page at the passengers. He had seen most of them before during his travels on the trains, which was indeed every day and night including week-end. It seemed that passengers always randomly choose the same carriages, especially during the rush hour. Usually most trains have eight carriages and he had been in almost all of the carriages, and each time, depending on which train or tube he was travelling on, the same people got on it and it goes without saying, they also alighted at same stations respectively.

On this particular day Roger was on the sixth carriage sitting opposite two blonde ladies who talked in a whisper to each other and tended to grimace after each sentence. This prompted Roger to pay close attention to them. Suddenly, almost what seemed like a premeditated action, one of the ladies got up and headed to the toilet in the carriage. He was flabbergasted when soon after she left, the other one followed and entered the same toilet while her friend was still inside. By this time Roger was entranced as he focused his gaze at the toilet's door in expectation that they would come out soon.

What started off as simple anxiety about the two blondes had suddenly turned into impromptu bewilderment and intense curiosity for Roger. It was obvious that the rest of the passengers were unaware of what was going on or perhaps they decided to be nonchalant which was typical of the Brits, they buried their heads between the pages of newspapers or clasped their mobile phones against their ears deep in conversation. The two blondes had been in the toilet for what seemed like ten minutes and he was wondering whether they would ever re-emerge as that would enable him identify their intentions. Then, without much ado, the toilet door opened, to Roger's astonishment, the two people that came out were men or dressed as men with dark hair, beard and moustaches. Roger's jaw dropped in astonishment, his eyes followed them as they moved on to a different carriage and sat down.

As the train hurtled into a station just before Richmond, the two alighted and to Roger's surprise they were met by two beautiful blondes who embraced them, hand in hand, the four exited the platform. Roger began to wonder if the blonde girls that welcomed the two were indeed females, in fact he was definitely curious as to whether the four of them were indeed males or females. However, he decided to perish the thought and wondered what would be the next drama as the previous passengers alighted and made way to new passengers who were entering the train in droves. As one lady entered, she made a bee line towards where Roger was sitting and sat in the empty seat which was next to Roger's seat. She was wearing a short mini-skirt and black tights. Her top half was barely covered by a very tight and transparent blouse which fully revealed her chest leaving her breasts almost completely exposed, her long black hair caressed her neck and shoulders whenever she turned her head side-ways. As soon as she sat down, she placed her little black leather handbag on her laps and opened it, rummaging through, she took out a little pouch containing a lip stick, small mirror and a brush and began to preen herself as the doors shut and the train continued on its journey.

Roger, however, uncomfortably focused at the lady wondering why she had to bring her make-up kit to use on the train. At this point several thoughts were conflicting in his mind such as 'why did she not apply the make-up at home or wait till she reached her destination? Just as the thought perpetuated and about to dominate his mind, it suddenly diminished into nothingness which was due to – perhaps that he had seen some ladies on the train applying their make-up, which was sometimes two or three ladies at the same time. It was more noticeable in the morning rush-hour, the difference was that the lady in question was indeed up front with it as soon as she entered the train.

As she preened herself, her phone rang, on answering it, she went into hysteria with laughter that turned heads in that carriage.

"Why did you call me chocolate box?" She said and chuckled into phone.

Then she roared with laughter again, oblivious to everyone on the carriage and heads turned again. Obviously no-one heard what was being said by the person at the other end of the phone. Roger began to wonder why he was subjected to such an excruciating discomfort with her sitting next to him.

"You could have me against the wall, by your desk or on the floor, I couldn't care less", she said loudly on to phone with a giggle.

At this point some of the passengers on that carriage suddenly focused their gaze disgustingly at her while some of the men loved her antics. In an instant she could feel that the vulgarisms that she had chosen were inappropriate, she slowly turned her head from right to left and noticed that most eyes were not only on her but also their faces were sternly, while some of the men were chocking with laughter. Unexpectedly, she rose from her seat, standing akimbo - she asked -

"What are you guys looking at? Have you not seen a pretty lady before?

A man standing near the carriage door yelled,

"Keep your conversation to yourself – will you?

Roger seized the opportunity and added,

"He meant, he is not interested in your antics"

She was rather infuriated at these comments and felt obliged to explain herself,

"If you must know – my name is Charli, my company moved to a new site and today happens to be our first working day at the site, my boss wanted to know where I would like my desk placed as I am his personal assistant, so, my reply was considerate – meaning that any available space would be okay" she paused,

"You guys should get a life – you know" she said with defiance.

"Good try, but do not expect me to fall for that," replied the man standing at the carriage's door.

This triggered thunderous laughter from the rest of the passengers on the carriage, eventually the train pulled up at Richmond station.

CHAPTER 3

Roger had been on the over-ground and the underground trains for some months and he was beginning to enjoy and appreciate the off-the-wall shenanigans and antics which were associated with life on the trains. Such were endless epic drama played out by varied actors without scripts to go by, the scenes were never written or rehearsed and the actors did not know one another, other than that they hopped on the train at different stations and were not even ready for any eventuality except being themselves whenever the occasion presented itself and that was when the stage curtains were drawn and the drama began to unfold.

The choice of who sat next to who could not be compromised because just being able to get a seat was the priority, some had met different gender or same gender of their dream as the case might be, and made friends and even some had got married to someone they met on the train while some had exchanged telephone numbers and got down to doing multi-million pounds worth of business. Some lasting friendships were also known to have been established too.

Roger alighted at Richmond station and made his way to the platform where he would catch the tube. Feeling peckish, he decided to get himself some snacks or something sufficient enough to pep him up before continuing on his travels that had no defined destination other than to kill time. He noticed a kiosk which was situated on the same platform where a small queue had formed and customers purchasing cups of coffee and some edibles, he proceeded to it and joined the queue waiting to place an order. A couple of minutes later a man and his lady companion joined the queue behind him. By this time, he ordered a cup of coffee and a bacon sandwich, searching his pockets he realised he only had enough money for the coffee which meant he could not have the sandwich, so he was about to return the sandwich when the man in the queue behind him tapped him on the shoulder,

"I will get that for you," said the man.

The man's lady companion giggled -

"If you were at the Victoria station about a few months ago you would not have this problem," she said.

Before Roger could object or accept his offer the man had placed some money on the counter,

"Take it out of this", the man said to the kiosk attendant.

"Thank you," said Roger as he stepped aside and began to masticate his sandwich.

When the man and the lady joined him as they waited for the tube train to arrive,

"Thanks again," said Roger.

"That's okay, it could happen to anyone," replied the man, "My name is Collin, Collin Smith,"

"Roger is my name how nice to meet you," said Roger.

Turning to the lady, Roger asked,

"What do you mean by 'if I were at Vitoria station I would not have that problem?'"

"Fifty pound notes rained down on the station, how I wished I was there," She replied with a giggle.

"At Victoria station?" Asked Roger.

"Yeah, a man launched a briefcase at the police, when it was blown up by a robot it played out the briefcase was filled with cash - all in fifty pound notes," replied the lady.

Roger suddenly became apprehensive and wondered if he had been recognised, the conflicting thoughts in his mind went into over-drive.

However, he decided to play it out.

"Why did the briefcase had to be blown up? Asked Roger.

"At first, we thought it was an explosive device, so it had to be detonated before any officer could get near it," said Collin.

"Why was the briefcase hurled at the police?" Asked Roger,

"I have no idea," replied Collin.

"It sounds mysterious as to why a briefcase full of cash was hurled at the police," said Roger.

"That was the mystery, we may get and answer when we find him," he paused "ironically his name was Roger" Collin added.

Just as the tube train was pulling up at the platform, Roger requested a business card from Collin and promised that one day he would be in a position to return the favour. Collin handed over his business card to him with a smile as he boarded the tube train with his lady companion while Roger entered a different carriage.

Although Collin did not seem to recognise that he had just bought a sandwich for the man he had been looking for, the man responsible for the briefcase incident at the Victoria station. On the other hand, Roger did not know that he had been talking with the police Inspector who was mandated to apprehend and interrogate him in that regard.

While Roger was sitting silently in the carriage reminiscing about his meeting with a complete stranger who had compassionately paid for his sandwich and coffee, the stranger who seem to have a comprehensive knowledge of the briefcase incident at the Victoria station. He wondered how this so called stranger came to know that the name 'Roger' was the name of the perpetrator. He removed the card that Collin had given him and glanced at it only to discover that the stranger was indeed a police inspector in charge of the case, he was gobsmacked as he descended into the abyss of monumental conflicting thoughts and invariably deeply entranced.

For the first time, he became completely oblivious to constant flux of series of drama which readily unfolded in the carriages. Strangely enough, Roger did not expect the briefcase incident to attract too many headlines let alone involve a police inspector.

After he temporarily resurrected from the thought in which he had been consumed, he suddenly noticed a girl staring at him with compassion, she was sitting up directly opposite him with both her hands between her thighs and her head tilting sideways. He was startled and he blinked as to ensure he was fully awake, after-all he had been entranced for too long since after his encounter with Collin and his female companion. Roger then realised that he was not dreaming, that the figure staring at him was real, his surprise gradually faded and gave way to astonishing delight. In a soft voice, he said hello to the girl,

"Hello" she replied softly with a smile that lit up her face.

"My name is Roger I am sure we have not met before" said Roger.

"My name is Soisin," replied the girl,

At this point both of them were lost for words as they starred at each other in silent admiration. She began to exhibit some nuance from her original composure by expressions subliminally of tantalising flirtation but with apparent innocence. They became the focal point of the passengers who sat close to them, pretending they were nonchalant to their electrifying attraction to each other.

Soisin is about twenty years old, slim and of average height, her eyes though fiery and big, portrayed tenderness and pure innocence.

Her rich long dark hair parted into two from the forehead and flowed down on both sides of her smooth and delicate chic bones to just over her shoulders, revealing a pointed nose and well-proportioned set of delicate lips. Her long dress lapped fittingly round her body as if she was born in it and it grew on her over time. Though she appeared slightly timid but that strongly enhanced her undisputed beauty. She was wearing a knee-length pair of boots.

She informed Roger that she was from a family of travellers, she was born in the United Kingdom of Irish parentage but accidentally parted company from her parents in the French Riviera of Monaco where she helped her parents in the family business, performing in the circus about three years before. One late evening in Monaco at the end of the circus, she went into the caravan, changed her clothes and went off with a girl whom she met in the field during the circus event. She confirmed that as soon as she saw Julianna, they had instant attraction with each other that she was convinced they would strike a strong and lasting friendship, so she stayed that night with her and then another night, and more nights after that without letting her parents know where she was.

After one week she returned to the caravan site to find that her parents had left the site and moved on without her. As she did not know where they had moved to, she went back to Julianna, she had not seen her parents and had no idea where they were since then.

"How come you are now in London? Asked Roger

"I came to London from Monaco one year ago," she replied

"And your friend? Asked Roger.

"Julianna arrived this morning from Monaco, so I am on my way to meet up with her," she replied, "You may come along if you wish," She added.

"Would love to - but I have no valid ticket for the journey," Roger replied.

"That's not a problem, just aim for your goal not the problems in between," said Soisin sternly.

Roger was taken aback at her philosophical positivity. He had not heard such a determined statement from anyone before let alone from an ordinary gipsy girl, the girl whom he thought was shy and timid had suddenly awakened with phenomenally striking wise words and he wondered if it was typical of gypsies.

Roger looked at her in silent wonder coupled with fuelled fascination and admiration for her undisputed beauty and apparent wisdom.

"Okay, I'll come along then" said Roger hesitantly.

Soisin told him that Julianna lived in Vauxhall, that she had been commuting between Monaco and London for the past two years, only at weekends, eventually she had decided to make London her home and she bought an apartment.

On their arrival in Vauxhall after changing trains, Roger was pleasantly surprised to find the ticket barriers broke down so it was needless to insert tickets in order to exit and no-one was checking for tickets so they exited meaning that he did not need to purchase a ticket after-all. At that point, Soisin reminded Roger how he was already creating problems for himself about not having a valid ticket and asserted that problems will always exist, that it is a part of life itself, but the intrinsic wisdom is to resolve them as one came to it and not to envisage it as a barrier or deterrent for one's goal.

"How do you come to know of all these? Asked Roger.

"Julianna thought me all that I know, she is wise and confident, also very compassionate and unassuming." She added.

CHAPTER 4

They left the station and continued walking towards the traffic lights on a busy main road which connected other roads near Vauxhall Bridge. They crossed the roads and emerged on the side walk at the other side of the road, to the right were some affluent development of delightful apartments which literarily dwarfed the surrounding buildings. To the front of the apartments flowed the River Thames unperturbedly in all its majesty. They climbed a couple of steps leading to the apartments.

"This is a very affluent neighbourhood" said Roger.

"Definitely so," replied Soisin, "she is a very fortunate person, you know what I mean, Julianna spends her time helping the less fortunate, also, she is serious with her Buddhist practice," She replied.

"How could she afford to live such life style, commuting from Monaco to London at weekends for two years and living in a place like this" Asked Roger.

"She made the cause for that, so it's the benefit of her good fortune," replied Soisin

It was late in the afternoon when they finally got into one of the buildings within the complex, Soisin pressed the inter-com and a soft voice was heard,

"Come straight up." Julianna's voice,

They entered the lift and proceeded to the top floor of a penthouse where she welcomed them at the door and led them in to a large living room.

Contrary to Roger's expectation, Julianna appeared to be quite a regular young lady, she appeared to be unassuming and she was wearing a pair of tight jeans trousers and a simple blouse that hung carelessly over her torso. She exuded confidence and Joy.

"Who is your friend? Asked Julianna".

"Roger" Replied Soisin.

"Pleased to meet you, Roger," said Julianna.

"It's my pleasure meeting you," Roger iterated.

Julianna seemed quite relaxed and composed which to Soisin, was not unusual of Julianna.

"How was life in Monaco? Soisin asked.

"Same as usual, never phased by any eventuality," Julianna replied.

"Nothing to be phased by, the weather is always conducive and the people are monumentally inspired by it – I suppose," said Soisin.

"Any contact yet with your parents? Asked Julianna.

"None whatsoever, I've been completely abandoned," replied Soisin with a giggle.

"Perhaps, they take it that a gipsy girl was capable of looking after herself." Said Roger.

"That's possible", said Julianna, passing a questioning glance from Roger to Soisin, "where did you two meet?"

"On the train," replied Roger.

There was a brief silence as Julianna momentarily gazed into nothingness, and then passed her gaze from Roger to Soisin as if consciously struggling to take solace from retrospective reality, she declared,

"My life was positively transformed by a young man I met on the train, as it turned out he became my first ever boyfriend, prior to that, I did not like men." Said Julianna as tears rolled down her delicate cheeks.

Roger and Soisin were totally astonished at Julianna's sudden nuance which was in the least not expected. Soisin began to wonder if there was deep misery beneath her outward exuberance and confidence, because in all the years she had known her she had never seen her in apparently despondent state. She could not wait to ask her whenever they were next alone together. She got up and hugged her intensely, at that moment Julianna went into a hysterical laughter and recomposed herself again.

"Sorry about this, I can assure you that my unexpected behaviour was a result of my previous sad life that inevitably transformed into the happy confident Julianna you are looking at now. I had no idea it would be possible but it certainly was." Said Julianna as her face lit up.

"Sad life? What sad life? Asked Roger anxiously

"Impossible to believe you'd a sad life," Soisin added.

"That was a long time ago, believe me it was sad and hard," said Julianna.

"How did you get over it, then? Asked Roger.

"Through my Buddhist practice." Julianna replied confidently.

"Buddhism? I thought Buddhism was to do with shaven heads, walking bare footed and relying on a strict regime of diet and meditation," murmured Roger sarcastically.

"You are certainly wrong," said Julianna assertively.

Julianna had not used her kitchen, she had just arrived same day. So, she picked up a 'take away' menu lying on the coffee table and asked them to choose whatever they would like to eat. That was music to Roger's ears because he had not eaten for almost two days except for the sandwich which Colin Smith paid for on the station platform.

After they had selected their meals, Julianna phoned the restaurant, placed the order and went into the kitchen.

Roger and Soisin went to the balcony to admire the Thames River flowing in its majesty with boats littered on it. They could also see the bridge nearby and the 'London eye' remained imposing in the distance. The houses of Parliament was also in full view across the river, it was a pretty sight. They were both silent as they were subjected to the astonishingly delightful view of London from Julianna's balcony and wondered what it would look like at night with the lights on.

Roger in contemplation, could not wait to ask Julianna what she does for a living which enabled her to afford such a pad in such a prime location.

A few minutes later, Julianna called them back to the lounge where she had coffee, tea and sumptuous slices of cake in wait.

A few minutes later just after they had tucked into the slices of cake, the intercom buzzed, it was the delivery man from the restaurant, he had brought their food.

No sooner he was let in than the dining table adorned with various kinds of dishes. It was at this point that Roger could not resist asking the question he had been putting off, he was trying to choose the right moment. Although, unsure if that was the right moment he decided to ask anyway. Soisin and Julianna were locked in a world of their own chatting about old times and Monaco which seemed to alienate Roger who was nonchalant anyway as he tucked into his meal.

Julianna, realising that Roger was left out in her personal conversation with Soisin, turned to him and enquired if the food he had ordered was palatable enough to which he acknowledged with a raised thumb, it was a sign of his approval that it was fine. This provided the opportunity for him to ask the question.

"This is a great pad, how did you manage to acquire it?" Asked Roger.

"Thank you for your kind words about my apartment," said Julianna

"Please do not misunderstand me, it's just that you are too young to own this lofty penthouse," said Roger defensively.

"Don't worry, you are free to ask me any questions." Said Julianna.

"My father bought this for me as a reward for changing from being a problem child to being the daughter he always loved." She replied.

"He had to be very rich to do that," said Roger.

"He owns properties and lands in the French Riviera, so, he had all the money he could ever need, but one thing that gave him happiness, I mean real happiness was that I changed from being a rebellious lost child to being his much loved daughter again,"

Tears began to roll down her cheeks again.

"You need to understand that I am not simply being emotional, it is actual tears of joy which brings us to the main story now. The real episode early in my life." Said Julianna

Roger and Soisin this time changed their seating positions and focused their gaze at her impatiently waiting to hear the story that had provoked tears in her eyes twice within a couple of hours each time she reflected into her past.

She begins to tell her story:

"I was an only child, mother past away when I was three years old and my father had to bring me up alone at the time when he was struggling with his business. The death of my mother gave him quite a hard knock as he juggled with having to bring me up properly, and having to cope with the enormity of stress triggered by working 'twenty four- seven' in order to rescue his business from declining."

"So he had no choice but to hire a maid full-time to look after me," she continued, "unbeknown to my father, the maid was leaning toward lesbianism, from that young age on, I had always been in the company of women and hardly saw my father as much as I wanted to.

23

Though he yearned to be with me most of the time but was restricted by his business engagements. Then, in my teens, my father wanted the best for me at all times, so I was sent to all girls' boarding school, the best there was in all the French Riviera."

"It was while I was in this school that hell broke loose, most of the girls there were in similar circumstances as myself, their parents wanted to give them the best education possible to prepare them for whatever challenges that life could throw at them and to excel in all fields of endeavour. Contrary to this belief, retrospectively, it seemed that the school succeeded in churning out girls that had no ambition in life, clearly the only qualification for being there was simply that one's parents were rich enough to send one there.

We got into all sorts trouble such as bunking from school and causing havoc in Nice and Monaco. It did not take long before we were all known to the police. My father was telephoned by them frequently that he spent ninety percent of his time coming to pick me up because the police had contacted him. It inevitably incurred more stress to his life. I got expelled from the school many times and was readmitted many times too. The principal of the school empathised with my father because she was aware of his almost helpless situation."

Roger suddenly got up,

"Could you pause for a while, Julianna," Roger requested

"Why?" enquired Soisin.

"I want to hear all of it." He replied as he hastily rushed to the lavatory.

Having realised they had not touched the food they had ordered as a result of strange captivation by Julianna's story, the two girls gazed at each other and burst out into hysterical laughter.

Roger emerged from the lavatory just as hastily as he went to it and noticed the girls were in hysterics.

"Have I missed something?" he asked

Soisin pointed to indicate full plates of food in front of them and said:

"We have not touched the food we ordered and they have gone cold now,"

"Please continue with your story Julianna," he pleaded.

"On one occasion during our escapade, we were at the beach in Nice when some guys approached us, it was on a summer's evening and the beach was reasonably busy but tranquil – I remember it well as if it were yesterday. Some people were just throwing some pebbles into the sea and watched them make ripples while others simply sat quietly soaking up the refreshing sea breeze. However, the 'naughty beach girls,' as we were notoriously called, spent most of our time by the beaches drinking and smoking, cuddling and kissing one another. Remember, a few of us had any experience with boys, we had always been in the company of girls some of who were already lesbians, although for a girl to fancy another girl may be normal but some of us had not discovered our sexual orientation, we were simply subjected to it by circumstances."

"So when the boys approached us at the beach, we smoked some stuff with them and had more drinks, the following morning, I woke up on a strange bed and since then, I was addicted to sex with boys, use of narcotics and drinking heavily.

For over one year, neither the school nor my father had any idea where I was, until one early morning, the police raided the house we squatted in behind a market stall and arrested all of us. It was at that time that the police tried to contact my father to learn that he had been hospitalised, his illness was induced by stress. It was simply obvious that I had caused it."

"Did you not have any relatives?" asked Roger abruptly.

"No, no uncles and the one aunt that I had lived in the United States, a retired journalist who was my father's sister, she had no children. My late mother was the only child and my father, the only male of two children. I hadn't the foggiest idea about my extended family, I left home too early and had not really been back since - so to say."

CHAPTER 5

"However, by this time I had made up my mind to visit my father at the hospital, so I caught the train from Nice heading to Monaco. I had lost a lot of weight and looked terribly haggard, the guy sitting right opposite me kept looking at me, I guessed he was genuinely sorry for me considering how wretched I looked. He said his name was Jodi, softly spoken, he looked confident, compassionate and warm, you could tell from his persona. Something about him that drew you closer to him and made you gain his trust instantly. However, when we got to Monaco he gave me his telephone number and simply said that he would like to see me again. On that train, he made me feel so adequate and relaxed. I very keenly wished to see him again, so, I was relieved and quietly ecstatic when he gave me his phone number."

"When I got to the hospital, I was taken to the private room where my father laid in bed gazing at the ceiling. He seemed unaware and I mean totally oblivious to his surroundings. As I stood at his private room entrance, tears rolled down my cheeks, he had emaciated almost beyond recognition, and then, I walked up to him and held his hand. Very slowly he tilted his head and saw me, at first he did not seem to recognise me and then he held my fingers as tight as he could, I noticed tears in his eyes as he groaned with delight at seeing me."

"On my next visit the following day, I discovered his condition had improved considerably in comparison to my previous visit, I was deeply gratified of which words were inadequate to express, the guilt that I felt previously evaporated, nevertheless, I still looked haggard and very thin indeed. He looked at me as if it was the first time he saw me since he became ill, his face was stern, then he shrugged his shoulders and said in a rather alarming voice"

"My daughter has turned into a vagabond, what happened, Julianna?"

"I did not answer the question because I knew exactly why he asked the question: 'what happened Julianna,' it's because I didn't look good, at-all."

"At the end of that afternoon, I phoned Jodi up and told him that I would like to see him. He had this ability to make me feel adequate and relaxed without even touching me, his humanity was extraordinary. That afternoon Jodi picked me up in his car in front of the train station as we arranged and took me to a Buddhist discussion meeting in the evening. It was only then that I knew he was a Buddhist. What I saw and heard at the meeting were eye opener, there were cross section of people, sincere and unassuming. At the end of the meeting, he gave me some books to read, the books contained the basics of Buddhist practice."

"After a number of weeks of practice, my father noticed the positive changes in me, I was happy and confident, so, I told him about the practice and he took it up. Needless to say – we are now one happy family. He has fully recovered and he is very happy too. He bought this apartment for me in the knowledge that I am now physically and mentally strong, as well as confident and happy. So, that was my story."

The silence that ensued was stunning that it could be cut with a knife and lasted for a good three minutes when suddenly,

"By God, you'd been in the wars!" exclaimed Roger, "So it was Buddhism that transformed you."

"Without a doubt," Julianna replied

"I should take up Buddhism myself, great stuff," said Roger.

"Really, every-one deserves happiness," usually there is always a meeting here some evenings if you would like to come along," Julianna said enquiringly.

"Sure," he replied emphatically.

Soisin looked at him, as if to reassure him, said

"I too will be here for the meeting,"

"I went to a public school, one of the best, but it's nothing like yours, we were well behaved except that we played hard during vacation, ironically, like you, I was also an only child," he said

"I never went to school," said Soisin

"Really?" Asked Roger

"Yes, really, gypsy culture, all the educating was done in the caravans as we moved along from place to place, that was enough I suppose," Soisin replied.

"So much for the wandering race – eh" Roger said.

"Do you regret it?" Asked Julianna

"Nothing to regret, it's our culture" replied Soisin.

All this time two of the dishes had been untouched but Roger had a couple of mouth fulls of his own dish. They had been consumed in Julianna's story that they ignored the sumptuous dishes that were delivered to them which had now gone cold.

It was late evening and the day was dawning rapidly, so, Roger asked if he could have a doggy-bag of his food. He had to go, in the hope that the train station would remain unmanned.

He was walking towards the door clutching his doggy-bag when Julianna got his attention and gave him a magazine to read whenever he had the time.

He briefly flipped over some pages there and then and glancing at a few lines,

he pointed out a couple of word that struck him which were, 'Winning life,'

"What is this 'Winning life' about?" he enquired.

"It's exactly about what it says 'Winning life'" replied Julianna

Could you tell me more about it?" He asked.

"How long have you got?" Julianna asked.

Returning to his seat

"Go for it," he said.

She begins,

"Each of us possesses the potential for a winning life. Within us is the ability to live with courage, to have fulfilling relationships, to enjoy good health and prosperity, to feel and show true compassion for others, and the power to face and surmount our deepest problems."

"How could one realise that? That is the question," he emphasised.

"Okay, crucial to living a winning life is to undergo an inner transformation that will enable us to bring out our highest human qualities and change our circumstances. This process is a revolution of our own character, an individual human revolution."

"So, how can we achieve that?" He asked.

The historical Buddha Shakyamuni Gautama discovered that all humans have the potential for enlightenment – or – 'Buddhahood' in the depths of their lives. This could be likened to a rosebush in winter: the flowers are dormant even though we know that the bush contains the potential to bloom". She continued, "considering your first question which was 'how could one realise that.'"

"Yes, that is the most important," He replied.

"By, tapping into our potential, we can fine unlimited wisdom, Courage, hope, confidence, compassion and vitality, so, instead of avoiding or fearing our problems, we learn to confront them with joyful vigour, confident in our ability to surmount what-ever life throws in our path."

"Buddhism also shows us the most satisfying way to live among others. It explains that when we help others overcome their problems, our own lives are expanded. When our capacity increases and our character is strengthened, the source of our problems comes under our control. Because we make an internal change, our relationship with our problem changes as well, wresting positive resolutions in any number of astounding yet tangible ways."

"Life is ever-changing, moment to moment. The only constant in life is change. Our minds are constantly in flux, and while one minute we may have the courage to conquer the world, the next minute we can be overwhelmed by even the simplest occurrences. But through our steady, daily practice, we continually strengthen our resolve and ability to win in life."

"To win in life, however, is not the absence or avoidance of problems, being human, almost by definition, means we will constantly meet up with challenges. True happiness or victory in life is having the tools to take on each hurdle, overcome it, and become stronger and wiser in the process."

Roger began to look at his watch intermittently. Julianna observed him but she continued in a haste.

"Inside each human being is a storehouse of all the necessary traits to tackle every problem that confronts us. Buddhism is the practice that allows us access to this storehouse and unleashes our inherent power to take on all life's challenges and win."

"Wow incredible, I need some of that," said Roger with fascination.

He got up and started walking towards the door to leave. Julianna took the magazine from him and wrote down her phone number:

"Give me a call soon, will you," she asked

"Great evening, we shall do this again," he murmured delightfully.

He opened the door and left.

As soon as he left, Soisin went to the kitchen followed by Julianna to warm up their cold food in the microwave.

"Does he live far?" Julianna asked.

"No, we met on the train on my way," said Soisin.

"I thought he was your boyfriend," said Julianna.

CHAPTER 6

When Roger got on the train there was only one thought in his mind, though, meeting up with Soisin and Julianna and having to spend almost a whole day in an opulent apartment was a welcome relief as he had not left the trains in a very long time. He was also quite happy to be in the company of two beautiful and free spirited ladies in whose company he felt so much at ease regardless that they were strangers.

However, he could not comprehend why the Inspector's picture was on the front page, since he was unable to read the text that followed very well because of how the man sitting opposite him was holding the newspaper, he decided to walk through the carriages to see if he could find a disposed Evening standard newspaper in any of the bins or perhaps, a discarded free paper that might be lying on a vacant seat so he could read the content in order to find out what the story was, about the Inspector.

He hurriedly walked frantically down the carriages towards the back of the train hoping to find a newspaper but to no avail. He turned round and was returning to his seat when the train pulled up at a station, here, the man who was sitting opposite him reading the paper got up and alighted leaving the newspaper where he was sitting. Roger made a Bee line at the paper and grabbed it.

The headline read: 'Police Inspector asked to resign or face compulsory discharge'

The story was that since Inspector Colin Smith was promoted four years ago, he had not successfully closed a single case, for that reason therefore, he was given one month to produce a successful result to any of the cases he was assigned to or resign, if not he would definitely be dismissed from the police force. At first, Roger was ecstatic about the News in the knowledge that he might be free from being arrested by him.

He spent the night on the train as usual, the following morning, for the first time since he left his home he telephoned his mother instead of dropping her a note as he did in the past. His mother was pleased for his phone-call, at least she knew he was alright but she pleaded unsuccessfully that he came back home. She informed Roger that the police had been swarming their home at odd hours asking both she and his father awkward questions about him and a briefcase that was hurled at police officers at Victoria station and whether he was connected with a drug gang.

Roger asked his mother if she knew the name of any of the police men, to which his mother mentioned without hesitation, 'Inspector Collin Smith.'

Right-away, Roger told her not to worry too much because the Inspector would not have his job very soon. His mother - Marie, became more and more nervous and repeatedly asked him why he ran away from home and why the police was looking for him, also about his connection with the briefcase in Victoria station.

He was evasive to her questions, instead he asked his mother about Erika, his childhood sweet heart whom he had not contacted since he went to live on the trains. His mother replied that Erika had been in the dark because he often visited to ask where he had gone to and when he would come back, that she was concerned and duly astonished for his silence for such a considerable length of time.

Then Marie suddenly saw Mr Dean - Roger's father through the sitting room window pulling onto the drive. She told Roger that his father had just returned from a meeting and urged Roger to hold on and speak to his father but he sounded indifferent and just asked Marie if Erika was alright. She replied that she looked alright except that she seemed to have lost some weight.

Roger rang off without waiting to speak to his father who had just walked in through the front door.

Erika had been to the shops and was on her way home when she saw a photo-fit by the electric pole, the photo-fit looked like Roger but since she was still in the dark of the circumstances about him and the briefcase she did not give it a second thought and continued walking home. As she put the key in the front door she could hear the phone ringing. She opened the door and rushed to pick it up but it rang off. She settled down to write his diary. She's been keeping a daily diary of how he missed Roger since his disappearance. Just as she finished jotting down what was in her mind, the phone rang again. She picked it up quickly, it was Marie at the other end,

"Hello Erika," Marie said,

"Hello Marie," acknowledged Erika, "did you hear from Roger?"

"He called a few minutes ago, he enquired about you with great concerned and affection." Marie replied.

"And…," Erika prompting her to continue.

"So, I told him that you are worried about him and that you've lost some weight," said Marie.

"Did he say why he did not want to call me?" she asked.

"He did not even want to speak to his father, he rang off after he asked about you, so, I phoned to find out if he had called you," said Marie

"Did you call before, about five minutes ago?" Asked Erika curiously

"No," replied Marie.

"I should leave the line free in case he calls, it could be him that called five minutes ago," Erika suggested.

"Most likely," said Marie.

Erika waited all day but there was no phone call from Roger. The following day, there was no phone call either, a whole week had passed, she did not hear from Roger, So she became despondent and resorted to pacing up and down her lounge still hoping that Roger would call her any minute but to no avail. Finally she frantically went for the diary that Roger had bought for her on her birthday. She thought the best way to use it was to record her daily activities which she would show to Roger when he returned on vacation from the University – that was before he disappeared. She really treasured the diary because it contained details of her daily activities. It was a difficult time for Roger's parents, nevertheless, Erika felt she was the one who got the raw deal due to the fact that she had not heard from him for several months which was from the time he disappeared. At least he contacted his parents sporadically. Only if she could hear his voice to know he was fine where ever he might be. Roger's whereabout was a mystery, for some reason they knew he was not far away and little did they know he had no fixed abode.

Roger was rapidly running out of money, the previous week, it was Colin, the police Inspector who failed to realise that Roger was the person who he was supposed to apprehend that paid for his sandwich and a cup of coffee and later in the evening of the same day he ordered a meal which Julianna paid for at her penthouse. He decided to get off at the next station to draw some cash. Rogers account was quite healthy but he did not see any reason for holding a lot of cash on the train as there was nothing to spend it on. Suddenly, he noticed two cute dogs on a leash at the other end of the same carriage that he was in, as he glanced at the two people at the other end of the leashes he realised they were supposedly the two blonde ladies who went to the toilet together on the train some time earlier and came out as men. He was fascinated as he fixed his gaze at them. He decided he would not get off at the next station as he previously intended. He made up his mind to follow them in other to know what they would be up to this time. Then the train stopped at the next station. Contrary to Roger's expectation, the two supposedly blonde ladies alighted with their dogs. Roger also alighted, he would be cashing some money from the cash point which was inside the station, and he did not have to leave the station, It was ideal for him because he had no ticket which would enable him to exit the station but his eyes followed the two supposedly ladies until they were out of sight.

He cashed some money from the cash-point and went back directly onto the platform to wait for the next train, on second thought, he decided to have some coffee since he was not actually going anywhere in a hurry and had no particular destination. He made his way to the coffee bar on the same platform and ordered a cup of coffee and a large muffin. He got what he ordered, picked up a newspaper, a different newspaper to the one he had read earlier and sat on one of the benches. He noticed that the front page headline was also about the Police Inspector Colin Smith, which read 'Go get them or be sacked,' with his picture underneath the headline. As he munched his muffin, he could not help asking himself 'what if the Inspector had recognised him the day he paid for his coffee and sandwich, would his or the Inspector's circumstances changed?'

Then suddenly a man wearing a hat and dark glasses appeared and sat on the same bench next to him. Roger noticed that this man was certainly agitated because he erratically stood up again, and then looked at his watch and sat down again, constantly glancing at his watch. However, Roger continued eating his muffin and drinking his coffee, he had no particular destination and certainly not in a hurry. He was just killing time before boarding another train, any train. The agitated man sitting next to him rummaged through his pocket, took out a phone and made a call, but it seemed there was a voice mail asking him to leave a message. The voice mail was quite audible that Roger heard it. He just exclaimed frantically, 'Bloody fool' and switched the phone off and put it back in his pocket.

When the train arrived the man got up, took out a tissue from his pocket and removed his dark glasses to wipe off sweat, he turned to Roger and said apologetically,

"Very sorry for my inappropriate language," as he was entering the train.

Roger was petrified because when the man removed his dark glasses to wipe off some sweat, he clearly saw his face and he was in fact - the Police Inspector, Colin Smith.

He had missed Roger for a second time even though it was only two of them sharing a bench and he still failed to recognise him. Roger was thinking if that was the case, he couldn't have been any good at his job or perhaps it could be because the headline disoriented him and obviously got him worried as the loss of his job was eminent.

On the other hand, it could be that it was because Roger had grown his beard and as such was not easily recognisable. He had been wearing the same clothes for almost one month and had not shaved nor had a proper bath except occasionally washing his face.

Then he remembered chatting with a tramp sometime before who gave him a tip of the particular stations that had bathing facilities, so he decided it was time he had a bath.

With that in mind, he changed direction and walked to a different platform. He had to have a bath.

Roger's parents, Mr Dean and Marie were having dinner in their dining room, the telephone rang, and Marie answered it. Holding the receiver in her hand she turned to Mr Dean.

"It's for you," she said.

"Who is it," asked Mr Dean.

"Your friend Dick," she replied, "shall I ask him to call back?

"It's okay, I'll take it," said Mr Dean

Mr Dean took the phone from Marie, she went back to the table and continued eating her dinner. Thirty minutes had past and Mr Dean was still on the phone, Marie was not too pleased that the dinner she prepared for herself and her husband has been compromised by a telephone call. She had now finished eating her meal and Mr Dean was still talking with Dick on the phone. They were old school chums and wore the same old school tie. Dick, a risk taker and a successful International Barrister, married a beautiful lady, also a Barrister, her name was Laura. She was originally from the Bahamas. After their marriage in London they moved to the Bahamas and established a successful law firm. Over time, Dick had become a compulsive gambler.

Eventually, Mr Dean returned to the table to continue his dinner but Marie was fuming with controlled rage because the sumptuous meal she had prepared had got quite cold. She quietly made her way into the lounge and sat down, Mr Dean obviously realised that Marie was very angry but nevertheless, he sat down and ate his cold dinner. When he had finished, he went to the lounge to join her but she was not in the mood to talk.

The silence was excruciating.

"You could have asked him to call back," said Marie angrily.

"I thought he was calling from the Bahamas," He replied.

"Where was he calling from then?" she asked

"He is here in London" he replied.

There was silence again for a while.

"Did he tell you he was coming to London?" she asked condescendingly.

"No," he answered.

"But he usually did," she said.

"Tell me about it," said Mr Dean.

"Something is not quite right," murmured Marie

CHAPTER 7

Few weeks had passed since the Newspaper headline about Inspector Colin Smith. He was eventually summoned to a meeting during which he was told that they were thinking of handing over the cases assigned to him to some other Inspector but they had decided to give him a few more weeks and then the progress would be reviewed after that. That meant that in order for him to keep his job, he had to pull his socks up.

Roger had read from the Newspapers that Inspector Colin Smith was also responsible for the case about a woman who trolled journalists and politicians with blackmail. She was a prolific operator and the police was determined to bring her to justice. Newspapers had shown a photo-fit of her but she was always one step ahead, despite the fact that Inspector Colin Smith and his team constantly received helpful information about the woman.

Roger had been on the train now for almost a year and had only been out of the trains or train station just ones. That was when he met Soisin and they went to see Julianna at her penthouse. After having a shave and a bath at the station's facility, he was looking quite fresh and revitalized. Only then he decided to read the Buddhist magazine which was given to him by Julianna at her penthouse, he did not put it down until he had finished reading it. The paragraph which explains 'the connectedness of one and his environment' and 'course and effect' particularly stuck in his mind which he underlined. When he put the magazine down, he accidentally saw Julianna's telephone number written at the back of the magazine and he immediately called her but the voice message asked him to leave a message.

"Hi Julianna, this is Roger, I hope you'll remember me," Roger leaves a message.

Then he called Erika, and got her voice mail, he chuckled with dismay and about to switch his phone off and then on second thought he left a message:

"Hi Babe, I miss you a lot," he paused, "could you go to my mother and collect my brown jacket, a Levi Jeans, and a couple of shirts for me, I'll call you again," requested Roger

After turning off his phone, he went into deep thought contemplating on what he had read in the Buddhist magazine, its principles totally and positively influenced his psyche in a very compassionate way and instantly gave him a new sense of responsibility. His understanding about life reached new heights and he became increasingly motivated to meet up with Julianna and Soisin to hear more of this Buddhist principles and to ask some questions. He seemed to have an *ad etic* memory and could remember all that he had read from the magazine. He certainly thought that the Buddhist principles made a lot of sense and that he could relate to them. For him it was an eye-opener that it was taking over his life for the better.

On Erika's return that evening, she played her answer phone and almost fainted, she had been expecting his call and waited all week for it but to no avail and the minute she walked out to get some grocery he called, and there was no mechanism on her telephone which would enable her retrieve the caller's number. So, she played the message over and over again to ensure that she understood all that he had said. She plonked herself on the sofa reminiscing how she and Roger used to walk hand in hand into shops and grocery stores to get some shopping together, but now she walked everywhere alone. Then she began to wonder why he had to disappear suddenly without warning, nor showed any signs that he would do so. The question of whether he did not love her enough did not cross her mind in the slightest as she yearned for him ceaselessly and couldn't spare another minute to reminisce, she quickly telephoned Marie, Roger's mother,

"Hello Erika, any news?" Marie enquired anxiously.

"Yes, he left a message," she replied.

"May I know what it was?" Marie asked

"Did he not call you?" Erika asked

"No." replied Marie

Erika therefore passed the message on to Marie about his Jacket, a pair of jeans and a couple of shirts which she would collect from her for Roger. Both of them suggested that perhaps Roger's return was imminent.

Marie assured Erika that the clothes would be ready for her to collect the following morning,

As soon as Erika put the phone down, she went straight for her diary and began to jot down her upward and downward oscillations of her feelings and emotions which was perpetuated by Roger's message to her.

That night, after Marie had prepared dinner for herself and Mr Dean, she went into Roger's room. All of his things remain as they were before his disappearance. She stood in the middle of the room and began to look round, from his bed to his book-shelf and to the pictures on the wall, visualising how he used to sit on the chair doing his studies and she would come in to let him know that lunch

43

or dinner was ready to which he would reply "thanks mum, I'll join you and Dad in a minute." Right now the same room is empty and no activity within it. She contemplated for a while and opened the wardrobe and began sorting out his clothes in accordance with his message.

Just as she had finished sorting them out, Mr Dean arrived, he had been to meet up with Dick for some private discussion which was by invitation from Dick.

Marie and Mr Dean had just settled at the dining table when the phone rang. Marie gazed at Mr Dean sternly implying that he should not leave the dinner table to pick the phone. He clearly understood the warning because last time it happened, his dinner got cold and Marie was not pleased. So, he did not move but continued eating his dinner, the caller rang off, a few minutes later the phone rang again and persistently. Marie stormed to the phone, picked up the receiver:

"Hello," said Marie sharply

"Could he ring you back? Asked Marie.

She put the receiver down, returned to the table and continued eating but with less appetite this time.

"It was Dick I guess," said Mr Dean with some reservation.

"Yes it was," she replied

"But I have just spent almost ninety minutes with him,"

"So, what was it about? She asked curiously.

"I think perhaps he is in a lot of trouble," he said, he couldn't get himself to tell me what it was, he was just going round in circles and could not spit it out."

"So he needs some help," she said

"I guess so, but he has not asked - yet" he replied

After dinner, Marie updated Mr Dean about Roger's message, he also thought like Marie and Erika that perhaps Roger's return was imminent but he was aware that it could be just a mere wishful thinking, however, he handed some money to Marie for Roger should he need it where ever he might be. So, Marie had parked the clothes in a rock sack waiting for Erika to collect in the morning, also the sum of money that Mr Dean had put in an envelope for Roger.

CHAPTER 8

Erika arrived at Roger's parents' home at the crack of dawn to pick up the items from Marie. Mr Dean was just getting ready to attend his surgery, being a dedicated parliamentarian. Marie brought the rock sack and the money and handed them to Erika and hurried to the kitchen to make a nice cup of coffee for Erika, at this time, Erika was going through the items to make sure they were correct. When she had finished counting them, Marie reappeared with three cups of coffee and placed them on the table. Mr Dean joined them for coffee. Erika had a quick sip of the coffee and stood up to leave.

"I have to go, in case he rang, I am always missing his calls," she said.

Before they could ask her to finish her coffee, she had already exited by the front door with the rock sack firmly on her back.

Meanwhile, Roger was on the train heading to London from Woking. Woking is a large town in the local government district, located in the west of Surrey. It is at the south-western edge of the Greater London Urban Area and is a part of the London commuter belt with frequent trains and a journey time of about twenty four minutes to London Waterloo station which was also a very busy hub.

He realised he felt really clean and fresh, therefore, a lot more contented than he had felt for a long time, the shave and the bath had apparently made a lot of difference. This time he was just completely relaxed, the train suddenly stopped between stations. He was not bothered, he had no destination and certainly not in a hurry for anything. Sitting by the carriage's window, he had a full view of the local architecture, some delightful properties littered the beautiful scenery against the backdrop of matured bushes and open woodland. Roger was thinking of how delightful the spectacle was that he wished the train would remain there for some time. He saw a London taxi slowly proceeding towards the property which was quite close to his window. In the back seat were a couple, a man and a woman. As the taxi pulled up at the front door of the property, the couple alighted, settled their fare and the taxi left and was out of sight. The couple stood at the front door, a young lady who was clad sartorially opened the front door and led them in and closed the door, and then Roger shifted his gaze to other opulent architecture.

Announcement came from the train's driver that they were held up because of a minor fault in the signal and confirmed that they would be departing shortly. Suddenly as if it was in the movie, the couple who earlier had entered gracefully into the magnificent property dashed out of the front door and were running at high speed, each clutching what looked like metallic boxes and files. The lady who welcomed them at the door was running after them, she was screaming frantically. It was a quiet area and no-one was seen in the street to assist her in catching them. From Roger's window, it was like a television screen, he witnessed the whole scene. The lady chased them until the couple were out of sight, she turned back still frantic as she ran back into the house. A couple of minutes later, the train departed for the next station, by this time Roger who was feeling on top of the world earlier rescinded into an astonishing abyss of confusion. Although he witnessed what had taken place between the couple and the lady who chased after them, and might have rightly guessed what might have transpired. Though he was still unsure as the scene he witnessed outside the property could have been different from what took place inside, for that reason he decided to have an open mind.

A minute later, the train hurtled into the next station and stopped. Lo and behold the couple who he had seen being chased by the lady were the first passengers to enter the train quite hurriedly in the same carriage that Roger was sitting. They were still clutching the metallic boxes and files and they were gasping for air. Roger was intently observing their every move. It seemed their intention was not to be close together, so on their entry they took different positions on the carriage. While the man was standing by the door, the lady companion went to the far side of the carriage and sat down. As Roger observed them for a while, the penny gradually began to drop. For all intent purposes their disguise slowly unfolded and he realised they looked familiar. Finally, the penny dropped, and without a shadow of doubt Roger was certain they were the two people he had seen a couple of times before. What he was unable to establish was whether they were either men or women since they were always in disguise or cross-dressed. First time that he encountered them, they were two blondes who entered the toilet on the train together and came out dressed as men. On the second occasion, they had a dog each and when they got off the train, Roger had followed them to the exit and then returned to cash some money inside the station.

The train was now within the South west region of London. All this time, Roger was curiously stealing looks at them and noticed that they intentionally remained reasonably calm except that they maintained subtle communication between them by signing each other through gesturing.

The next stop would be the stations that was close to one of the busiest hubs in London, and this time the one that was sitting down calmly stood up and signalled the other one who was standing at the carriage's door with a nod of the head, within minutes the train entered the station and stopped. Without hesitation the couple got out and began to make their way to the exit. Roger followed them even though his plan was not to get off there. He was determined to follow them to their final destination incognito. They left the station, and walked down about two streets from the station then turned into a drive to an Edwardian semi-detached house. On the drive were a gleaming Jaguar car and a two seater Mercedes sports car. They looked sideways and backwards and then put the key in the front door and went in. Roger, who was covertly trailing behind but at the other side of the road was intentionally playing with his phone as he passed the imposing semi-detached house in which the couple entered.

He walked to the end of the street and turned into another street parallel to the one he had just left and returned to the station. He was not surprised to find out that it was at the same station that the couple alighted last time they had dogs with them.

Roger was on the platform waiting for the next train, as usual there was no destination. Announcement came through on the station's speakers that the next train would be twenty minutes late. So he decided to have a sandwich and a cup of coffee before deciding which way to go next. So he made a Bee line to the Kiosk on the same platform and ordered a sandwich and a cup of coffee and sat down to eat, when his phone rang, he had forgotten to switch it off like he usually did, because he did not want anyone to call him or to know where he was. However, on answering the phone he was pleasantly surprised that it was Julianna, he recognised that voice clearly.

"Hello, I retrieved your number on my phone but you did not leave a message, so I am trying to find out who it was," said Julianna

"Pleased to hear from you," replied Roger

"Who am I talking to?" She asked

"Roger, I've been to your house with Soisin, remember?" He asked

"Yes, I do remember," she replied, "I travelled to Monaco for two weeks,"

"How is Soisin?" he enquired.

"Very well, I am expecting her this evening," she replied

"I have read the magazine …huh… thought-provoking to say the least," said Roger

"Yes, we have a study meeting about the basics of Buddhism if you'll like to come," said Julianna

"Sure, I will be there," he said

"7.30 pm … right?" she said

"Right," He replied, "see you then."

Roger was indeed looking forward to meeting up with Julianna and Soisin again after a long absence and was overly excited to learn more about Buddhism.

He glanced at the time displayed on the information notice board, it says 3.00 pm, which meant he had some time to kill before heading off to Julianna's penthouse. He was somehow enchanted that he had a useful destination to go to for a change. He settled down on the bench and enjoyed his sandwich and a cut of coffee.

He was able to arrive at Julianna's penthouse just before 7.45 pm, which was about fifteen minutes later than scheduled. The door was opened for him by a young man. His first impression on entry was that he was warmly welcomed by this young man who made him feel very comfortable and it re-assured him that he was not out of place regardless that he was new, and his first time to attend such a meeting. He also noticed that Julianna's lounge was already full of people, all of them faced and focussed at a scroll which was in a box centrally placed on an elevated platform at the other end of the lounge. He also noticed they were all reciting some words in a foreign language. He simply sat down at the back and waited. As he looked around, Soisin and Julianna were the only two people that he recognised. At the end of the recitation, they began to chant some phrase for a few minutes and then stopped. From the introduction that followed, he realised it was a good cross-section of the community, more like the United Nations assembly with an eclectic mix of occupations and nationalities, ranging from lawyers, teachers to nurses, students, jobless people, writers and artists, men and women, young and old. Definitely they all seem to be happy and at peace, and oozed warmth and joy. It was astonishingly extraordinary to Roger who found such aspects most significant and positively awesome.

During the discussions, Roger was particularly interested in the general discussions about the basics of Buddhism. Other topics were that every individual is a macrocosm of the universe, that is, everyone is a mini universe:

> *Our lives exist, have always existed, and will always exist simultaneously with the universe. They neither came into being before the universe, occurred accidentally, nor were created by a supernatural being. Nichiren Daishonin (the Buddha of the later day of the Law) taught that life and death are the alternating aspects in which our real self manifests itself, and both are part of the cosmic essence.*

The following quote by the mentor and teacher Daisaku Ikeda remain indelible in his mind.

> *"When we care for others, our own strength to live increases, when we help people expand their state of life, our lives also expand. Actions to benefit others are not separate from actions to benefit oneself. Our lives and lives of others are ultimately inseparable."*

At the end of the vibrant and sincere discussions at the meeting, Roger was so enthused with the genuine revelations of real concerns about life in general, he was resigned to deep thought about his own personal mission. Being a bright student he wondered if William

Shakespeare was right in the way he wrote. Shakespeare's analysis about life struck a chord in his heart, especially the following Shakespearian lines:

> *"Life is but a working shadow, a poor player*
> *That struts and frets his hour upon the stage*
> *And then is heard no more."*

However, Buddhism emphasised that whatever one's present circumstances might be right now, was exactly the right platform for one to take responsibility for creating one's happiness and also to help others achieve the same. One will inevitably become happy irrespective of one's present circumstances when one chants Nam-myo-ho-renge-kyo.

He was beginning to think that perhaps his odyssey was his own platform, if that was the case, he had to re-evaluate how to create value on that platform.

CHAPTER 9

The following morning, Roger was on the train as usual and he overheard some passengers as they were engaged in what seemed a serious
discussion about stolen jewelleries and sensitive files. He did not pay
any attention because, it was not unusual on most train journeys for
colleagues and friends to discuss a lot of topics ranging from stock
market to the antics in the offices, family feuds to TV and Theatre
plays they had watched the previous night, an eclectic mixture of
topics. Suddenly, a young man sitting on top of what looked like
an enormous tool box right by the carriage's door started talking
into his mobile phone in a very loud voice, he was oblivious to other
passengers on the carriage. After ranting and yelling for about three
minutes into his phone without due consideration to others, the rest
of the passengers that were having private chats suddenly stopped as
the young man's voice continued echoing throughout the carriage, and
still he was nonchalant. Then he seemed to have reached a crescendo
when he burst into a hysterical and infectious laughter - all alone.
At this point, the passengers' anger which was initially subdued,
immediately turned into ecstatically loud and uncontrollable laughter
too and before long, everyone in that carriage was laughing, it was
a melodramatic incident. The irony was that no-one understood a

single word the young man was saying. He was speaking in a foreign language and yet he provoked thunderous laughter from everyone.

Roger alighted at the next station, he felt a strong desire to call his girl-friend Erika, but before he could do that, he felt the nature's urge to pay a visit to the gents' toilet. In this toilet, he came face to face with a tramp who was breaking up stubs of half smoked cigarette he had picked up from various rubbish bins, as he broke the stubs up he tipped the tobacco from the stubs into a tobacco rolling paper, rolled it up and smoked it. The tramp did not recognise Roger at first glance but on the contrary he was immediately recognised by Roger. He was the same tramp that gave Roger useful directions about where to shave and where to get a bath on the London train stations.

Roger said 'hello' to him and thanked him for the useful information he availed to him. When he had finished using the toilet he opened his wallet and handed over a twenty pound note to the tramp. That was overwhelmingly jaw dropping to the tramp who might have not seen or held a pound coin in years let alone a twenty pound-note.

Roger left the gents toilet, picked up a free daily newspaper from the newspaper bin, proceeded to the platform and began to peruse. The headline featured a couple alleged to have forcibly taken two boxes full of jewellery, maps and plans of all the listed properties and files containing personal details of members of the public. The time and location corresponded with the incident that he had witnessed from the train carriage's window. He then quickly read the rest of the article with curiosity to learn that the couple posed as very important buyers of listed properties and had come to view the grade two property, the victim was a Lady Greenstables. She lived in the property with her husband Lord Greenstables who was away on a very important meeting in Geneva.

Consequently, the article he had just read became food for thought for Roger, he had witnessed the whole incident very closely from his carriage's window while he was comfortably relaxed on the train. He wondered if he was the only passenger who witnessed the incident unfolding. If he reported to the police that he saw the incident that unfolded, he would be required to be a witness and that meant blowing his cover, if he did not report to the police, the culprits might never be caught. With these conflicting thoughts in his mind he decided to call his girlfriend Erika instead. After-all, he needed a change of clothes.

He rummaged in his jacket pocket and retrieved his phone and called Erika but there was no answer. He switched off his phone, picked up the newspaper again and continued reading. He called Erika again and again but to no avail, so he called his mother Marie and asked if Erika had collected his clothes. Marie told him that she had collected all the clothes that he had asked for some time ago and added that she was surprised that he had not collected them from Erika. This time Mr Dean was at home and overheard Marie talking to Roger on the phone, he approached Marie and gestured to her to give him the phone so he would speak to Roger

"Hold on Roger, your father wants to speak to you," said Marie

She handed the receiver to Mr Dean.

"Hello son, what explanation do you have for abandoning your mother and I."

"I have neither reason nor explanation, Dad," Replied Roger.

Mr Dean was still holding the receiver in his hand and about to continue talking with him when Roger suddenly hung up. Mr Dean turned to Marie who was standing behind him and said:

"He hung up on me,"

"Because you keep asking him the same question," replied Marie

"Why has the police not found him?" he asked

"Perhaps he is smarter than you think," she replied sarcastically.

Two week had past but Roger did not see the couple again on the train. He thought that it could simply be a ploy by staying low until the dust cleared, then he thought of Inspector Colin Smith: if he would be assigned to the case. On second thought, he would not, because he only had a couple of weeks for him to be reviewed for his job. Roger was thoughtful for a while contemplating on what to do next. He irrationally dashed to the nearest public telephone box, took out the card that Inspector Colin Smith had given him the day he paid for his sandwich and coffee at the Kiosk on the station's platform. On this card were two phone numbers, one was his office number and the other his mobile number. So he called his mobile number and got a voice mail, so he left the following message:

> "Hi Inspector, as they say, a smile costs nothing but it buys a lot. You may not know me but you paid for my sandwich and coffee sometime ago on a train station's platform when I did not have enough money to pay for them. I know you may lose your job in two weeks' time after your review but you need not worry. I will save you from that. Will call you again."

He hung up.

Coming out of the public phone box he made sure no-one was watching him. The only person he had ever called on his phone was Erika and her mother having warned them that if they gave the police his phone number or informed the police that he phone them, they would not see him again and would not contact them anymore. He was taken precaution earlier when he only contacted his mother in writing. In this regard, his mother had not told the police about Erika, therefore, Erika was completely out of the picture. Roger did not want the police to find him or trace his calls to know of his whereabouts. For that reason he had to constantly turn his phone off when it was not in use.

He caught the next available train and continued on his journey that had no particular destination. It was very late at night, the train was almost empty so he found time to relax and reminisce about the buddhist discussion meeting he had attended earlier and wished to tell Erika all about it and perhaps she might like to go to the next meeting with him. The train reached the end of its journey that night. Roger realised he was not the only person still on the train as he peered through the adjoining doors into the next carriage, he saw someone who seemed not to be in a hurry to leave the train. The man was wearing a three piece suit and tie and carrying a briefcase. Curiosity got the better of him, so he walked over to the carriage and proceeded to where the man was sitting. To his astonishment it was the tramp whom he had given a twenty pound note in the gents' toilet. He could not believe what he had just seen, the tramp who always wore dirty trousers and dirty overcoat and carried a worn out rag bag, the same tramp who was unshaven and always loitering in the underground and train stations. As soon as the tramp saw him he understood perfectly well why Roger's jaw dropped when he recognised him.

He invited Roger to sit down: still confused and in shock Roger slowly and hesitantly sat down opposite the tramp. Just at that moment something dropped from the tramp's hand on to the carriage's floor. When Roger took a close look at the object when the tramp tried to pick it up quickly so that Roger would not identify what it was. Unfortunately the Tramp was too slow in doing so because Roger saw the object clearly and it was a police badge. Realising that Roger had seen and recognised his police badge, he forced a cheesy smile and was obliged to divulge his identity.

"Do you know, I did think you were one of us," said the tramp

"What do you mean?" Roger asked

"That you were a police officer until you gave me the twenty pound note, which meant that you actually thought I was a tramp" he replied.

"In what sense? Asked Roger.

"You should have known I was not a tramp, although you've no destination like some of us but that gave you away, now you know I was not a Tramp,"

Extending his hand to Roger for a hand shake,

"I am Detective sergeant Jake" said the Tramp

"Hi Jake, or shall I call you Detective sergeant? Asked Roger

"Jake is fine, I did not get your name," said Jake

"Oh, I am just a student," said Roger

"But there are no schools on the train," Jake said sarcastically.

"Just collecting stuff for my thesis, I am writing about trains and stations, that's why I did not have a destination," Roger said.

At this point Roger's quick thinking turned the table, he was the one asking the questions while Jake had to answer them.

"So what was a Detective sergeant doing in the toilet? Roger asked

"In my job, you could be on duty anywhere." Replied Jake

"So who are you after?" asked Roger

"If you read the papers, we are after all of them, replied Jake

"The jewellery and file thieves? Asked Roger

"Yes, and also the Victoria station incident …erm … and the woman who trolled journalist on the internet," replied Jake

Having mentioned the Victoria station incident, Roger knew it was time he departed.

Extending his hand for a hand shake with Jake.

"I have to catch a taxi home, it is already late," said Roger

"Okay, good luck with your thesis."

Roger aimlessly proceeded to the door and about to alight when Jake said with a growl:

"Remember, there is no school on the train,"

With these words from Jake, Roger suddenly felt some unsettling sensation deep in his stomach. He began to wonder if he had been following him all that time, whether he already knew he was the person responsible for the Victoria station incident. If Jake did know, there was a strong possibility that Inspector Colin Smith would also know, after-all he was Detective sergeant Jake's boss. That had an unexpected shocking effect on Roger which resulted in him leaving the train at the spur of the moment and walked to another train station in the opposite direction.

CHAPTER 10

Roger slept on the train that night as usual, the following morning Erika was still in bed when Roger telephoned her at the crack of dawn. The phone was ringing and Erika got up from her bed and walked sheepishly to the phone and picked it up,

"Hello," said Erika who was still half asleep

"Hi babe, it's me, Roger – very sorry to wake you," said Roger.

"Hello-oo babe, where are you?" Erika asked excitedly.

"Could you bring my clothes to 'Sloane square? He asked

"Okay, will be over right away," she said.

"Not right now, but at 3pm – platform one," he said

"Will do babe, love you lots,"

"Love you too," she blew a kiss on to phone and rang off.

She grabbed a pen and made some entries in her diary. She did not intend to go back to sleep so she sat on his bed reminiscing about what had just transpired. She then considered calling Marie to tell her the news but decided to wait a little longer in case she was still in bed. She opened her wardrobe and selected her favourite dress and put it down on the settee. She would wear it when going to meet Roger at Sloan square.

Erika was so much looking forward to meeting with Roger that day as if it was her first date with him. She checked her diary was complete and in order.

At 3pm Roger was waiting on platform one at Sloane square station fully geared up in anticipation to meeting up with Erika, wondering how much she would have changed after all that time they had detached from each other.

Meanwhile, Erika had dolled herself up and was wearing her favourite dress, with a rock sack that contained only Roger's clothes hung firmly on her back, while at the same time clutching her hand bag in which she put her diary. She gazed at her wrist watch and the time was 3.05pm, she was already in front of Sloane square tube station and about to cross the road and enter the station when a lady who was exiting the station snatched her hand bag and took to her heels along the road. Erika screamed and chased after her with the rock sack on her back. Out of the blue, a man on a motor bike appeared right from the corner of the shops and called out 'Charli,' to the lady being chased by Erika, Charli then jumped on the back of the motor bike with the hand bag and they sped off.

Inside the station's platform one, Roger was pacing about and glancing at his watch at regular intervals, the time then was 3.20pm. He was becoming despondent because he was aware that it was quite uncharacteristic for Erika to be late for more than ten minutes since they started dating. In fact in all that time she had only been late once. She had absolute trust in Erika therefore, he was hopeful that she would turn up eventually. So he continued pacing the length of platform-one, throughout this period many tube trains had arrived and departed. Then, suddenly, a young woman appeared from the other end of the platform, she was looking left then right, back and front. She appeared frantic, confused and stressed, oblivious to the presence of the waiting passengers she shoved her way to and fro looking for Roger. Neither of them was aware of the presence of the other on that platform. Finally, she started calling out in a loud voice, Roger! Roger! Roger!!

Now almost all the people on the platform joined her in calling out 'Roger' as they gawked at her. Roger was astounded to hear everyone yelling out his name and he began to proceed to the other end and then his eyes and those of Erika's met. They ran towards each other from the opposite ends of the platform into a very firm embrace which they held out for about seven minutes before extricating themselves from each other. They were the primary focus of everyone on the platform.

Roger slowly and carefully released the rock sack from her shoulders and put it on his. They kissed passionately and then clasped their hand around each other's waist and slowly strolled out of the station, not a word exchanged between the two throughout the incident.

They proceeded directly to the 'Rock-on,' their favourite restaurant in Sloane square where they frequented before Roger's disappearance, and immediately noticed that it had changed a great deal to their dislike, the usual charm and friendly ambiance with which it was reputed had disappeared. None of the staff that they were familiar with was there. It was quite apparent that it had changed management and now cater for the upwardly mobile clientele who like to flaunt their cash and talk about the stock market, and super cars. The warm and friendly exuberance that were the characteristics of the Rock-on Restaurant had significantly diminished. However, they were able to find a comfortable table-for-two close to the window facing the road.

Erika got up and went to the ladies' lavatory which was at the far side of the restaurant while Roger was going through the wine list and menu. Few minutes later she returned in a hurry trembling and frightened. She was trying to say something to him but couldn't get the words out, she continued trembling and pointing to the direction from which she had just returned,

"What's the matter babe?" He asked anxiously.

Erika was still struggling to say something and emphatically pointing in the same direction. Roger was sure she wanted to tell him something but the fright in her face was indescribable. So he stood up and gave her a tight hug,

"What's the matter?" he asked again

"She is…she is …over there" she said as she gasped

"Who is over there?" he asked

Roger took her by the hand and was leading her to the direction in which she was pointing when suddenly the couple that Erika was pointing at quickly left their table, went to the till and paid for their meal with a credit card and were fast heading toward the front door. That was when the words eventually came out of Erika's mouth,

"She is the one that snatched my handbag," she yelled

This alerted the dinning customers to the pandemonium that was unfolding before their eyes.

"Snatched your handbag?" Roger asked

"Yes," She replied.

"When?" he asked.

"Few minutes ago," she replied

By this time the couple quickened their steps, followed by a quick dash outside to the front of the restaurant, jumped on a motor bike and made a daring escape through the busy street.

It was the same motorbike that was used in the escape earlier when she snatched Erika's hand bag.

Consequently, in the commotion, the customers peered through the restaurant's windows to witness the ominous escape.

Roger quietly guided Erika back to their table where she told him the details of the incident,

Now Roger was able to understand why she was late at the station. Considering the effect it would have had on her, she was relentless and determined to see Roger, she did not show nor express despondency in any way. Her only concern was to see Roger. Her regret was that the diary she painstakingly prepared for him was also in the handbag that was snatched. She told him about the diary which she meticulously kept with the intention of giving it to him so that he would understand what she did since his departure.

As a result of what had played out, neither Erika nor Roger had any appetite for the meal they were about to order, however due to the fact that it was the only proper food that Roger would have in a long time, he was determined to celebrate their meeting with the meal so he persuaded Erika that in spite of what she had been through that day, they had to have a meal. After much persuasion Erika relented and they ordered their meal. After having their sumptuous meal, Erika looked at him sternly in the face,

"Why have you forsaken me for so long? She asked

"Wrong, you've always been on my mind," he replied

"But why are you doing this?" she asked

"What do you mean?

"Leaving home and not let anyone know where you were," she said

"The truth is that I do not know why, please believe me," he replied

"Are you going to come home with me now? She asked

"Not yet, I have a lot of work to do and I feel quite at home on my travels," he replied.

"So you expected me to be waiting for you indefinitely?" she asked

"But I have also been waiting for you all this time,"

Then there was silence, each of them descended into deep thought. Just at that moment a customer who had witnessed the incident earlier walked up to their table and placed a note and told them that it was the number of the motorbike that the couple used in their escape. He had noted the registration number when he peered out of the widow. Roger thanked him and put the piece of paper in his pocket.

Roger told Erika that for some reason he had seen the woman who snatched her handbag somewhere before. Erika told him that perhaps the woman's name was 'Charli' because that was the name the man on the motorbike called out just before she jumped on his motorbike at the time she snatched her handbag. That jogged Roger's memory, he realised that she was the same woman he had met on the train, the woman who wore short skirt and tights and a blouse that revealed most of her chest, the same woman who told the passengers on the carriage that her name was Charli as she carried on with her antics. She also told the passengers that they should get a life. So as soon as Erika mentioned that name 'Charli', the penny dropped, Roger was then certain where he had seen her before. They sat in the restaurant for an interminable period of time, their hands resting on top of their table and their fingers intertwined and clinched with each other's without saying a word as they gazed into each other's eyes. The day was drawing to a close when Roger stood up and helped Erika got up from her chair, still no word from either of them. They made their way outside the restaurant where Roger hailed a taxi for Erika and just before she left in the Taxi she said to him:

"So you do not wish to come back with me?

"Don't worry babe, I have to find your diary first," he replied

When the taxi pulled away with Erika, Roger carefully slung the rock sack upon his back and made his way back to the tube station.

The following morning, Erika was in a state of elation and damn right down-cast, the former because she was able to see Roger and the later was that she lost her diary. She was not really perturbed for losing her hand bag, it was losing the diary that she was concerned about. As a result, she had no diary in which to note down her experiences with

Roger. So, she telephoned Marie to tell her of their experience during the meeting.

"We had lunch in our favourite restaurant," said Erika

"Did he tell you where he's staying?" asked Marie

"No," replied Erika

"When he is coming home?" asked Marie

"No, Yes, when he finds my diary," replied Erika

"When he finds your diary?" asked Marie

Erika told Marie how she lost her handbag and how they saw the culprits in the same restaurant and how the couple made a quick getaway. Marie also enquired if Roger looked alright and in good health to which Erika positively confirmed.

Marie also asked her if Roger was still wearing his light blue jacket and black jeans to which Erika also confirmed. Marie was deeply concerned that he had worn the same clothes for about a year and she was not pleased in the slightest. However, she hoped that he would be able to change his clothes now that he has got some to change with.

CHAPTER 11

Meanwhile, inspector Colin Smith had received Roger's message and was fascinated by it, but he was also very careful in case it was a prank, nevertheless, he was immensely curious to hear from the caller and was expecting another phone call as was promised in the message. Despite the fact that his review was drawing very close he was still assigned another case, the case was about a man and a woman who were going round on a motor bike snatching handbags and mobile phones. Apparently the incident had happened to many people in different places. This had kept Inspector Colin Smith on his toes, and yet none of the cases assigned to him had had a closure or even near having a closure. The activities of the motorbike couples had spread like wild fire and became headlines on most newspapers.

Roger had changed his clothes and was really looking quite fresh, clean and trendy, it instilled more confidence in his personality, most of all he was not as conspicuous for wearing the same clothes as he was before. Sitting on a train perusing through a free newspaper, as he turned one of the pages he was overwhelmed with anger to see the feature on the motorbike couple. He read on and was astounded to learn that the couple who were responsible for snatching Erika's handbag were actually professionals and had victimised a lot of people in the same way as Erika. So, in retrospect he had witnessed two diabolical incidents, in a short period of time, firstly, the incident involving a couple who stole the two metallic jewellery boxes which he saw clearly from his carriage window and secondly, the incident he was just reading about. This very one affected him almost directly because it was the incident in which his girlfriend was a victim. In that regard he was determined to do whatever that was necessary to apprehend and remove them from the streets, he might even recover Erika's diary by leading the police to their arrest.

Roger got off the next station and called Inspector Colin Smith from a public phone booth, when the Inspector picked up the phone, he was disorientated by an urgent information that had just arrived from the police headquarters. Inspector Colin Smith therefore, put the phone down but did not hang up or switch the phone off, he had taken another call on a different phone. While he was talking to his colleague, Roger was listening and the information from Inspector Colin's colleague was clear and audible. It was about the motorbike couple, they had struck again and Roger could hear every word that was said. When Inspector Colin had finished talking to his colleague, he picked up the previous call and said,

"Hello, sorry to keep you waiting,"

"Never mind, it's me again," said Roger

"Could you tell me who you are?" he asked

"Remember paying for a sandwich and a cup of coffee for a total stranger? Roger asked

"At a kiosk on a train station plarform? Asked the Inspector

"Yes, listen carefully, go to no 131 Jagmer street, the Jewellery and file thieves live there." Said Roger

He replaced the receiver.

The Inspector then slowly and thoughtfully replaced his receiver and started pacing to and fro with both his arms crossed behind his back and in deep thought. Then he stood still for a while and then grabbed his jacket, got in his car, he was heading to no 131 Jagmer Street. After-all, there was nothing to lose and it is better to have tried and failed than to have not tried at-all, so, he was not prepared to ignore that opportunity no matter how trivial it might be. When he got within close proximity of the address he sat in his car watching the house. In the drive were a new Jaguar and a Mercedes sports car but there was no sign of life both inside and around the house. He waited for a considerable time and just as he was about to leave what seemed like men, two of them came out of the house and proceeded in the direction of the train station.

Unbeknown to the Inspector, Roger was standing in the distance watching him having had intuition that the Inspector would go to investigate the address. So, he went near the address before him and laid in wait. It was a big case that were headlined in all the national press, the case also victimised the captains of the civil service, and therefore, it was crucial that the perpetrators were brought to justice. Roger was determined to lead the way but incognito, and was all out especially to assist Inspector Colin Smith to bring the case to a successful closure.

As soon as the Inspector got back to his office Roger called him again from the public telephone,

"Inspector Colin Smith," answering the phone

"Those two that got out of the house were the culprits, said Roger

The Inspector was astonished beyond measure and wondered how he knew that he was at Jagmer Street, and that two people got out of that house, he stuttered on the phone,

"Who are you? Err.. What's your name?" Asked the Inspector

"Now that you've seen them, it is your job to arrest them, go on," said Roger confidently, "after this one, I'll give you another assignment."

He replaced the receiver.

The Inspector was still holding his receiver with dropped jaw, dumbfounded about the mystery caller, nevertheless, he was gradually being persuaded to believing him due to his actions and confidence. After a brief contemplation, he decidedly replaced his receiver and hastily called his men in for a brief.

CHAPTER 12

Two weeks later, Roger was feeling peckish and headed to a Cafe on one of the station's platforms, he ordered a plate of spaghetti bolognaise and settled down to read a free paper. He considered free newspapers indispensable as they were the only medium through which he updated himself with current events and gossips. Since he had been incommunicado, he totally relied on the free papers and a single day would not expire without him perusing them. On one of the pages he noted the headline which read that the Jewellery and files thieves had been arrested, as he read through, he learned that the couple were arrested the previous day by Inspector Colin Smith and his team. Words were inadequate to express Roger's delight about the arrest, he was filled with joy and a sense of fulfilment for being the catalyst for the successful arrest of the couple.

Following the auspicious news, he sat back in his seat mesmerised. Suddenly a tramp walked up to where he was sitting and asked him if he could spare him thirty pence for a cup of tea. Roger sat up again and gazed at the tramp with some sort of misgiving. Then the tramp said "if you do not have thirty pence, twenty pound note would do." On that note both of them roared in laughter, Roger had realised that it was Detective sergeant Jake, the so called tramp that he gave a twenty pound note in the toilet, he was wearing his covert tramp outfit. He deliriously joined Roger at his table.

"There are no schools on the train," said Sergeant, reminding Roger of his last words to him last time they met. Roger noted the sergeant's cue and both of them laughed uncontrollably.

"You have been following me," said Roger

"I saw you come in," said Sergeant Jake

"Tell me, who are you after, this time? Asked Roger

"Not the Jewellery and files couple, they've been detained," he replied

"How did that happen?" asked Roger

"The usual way, one Inspector Colin's team pulled them up for traffic offence, when they failed to stop, it resulted in a car chase along the M25. Finally they were caught which lead to their house being searched," said Sergeant Jake

"Any evidence found?" Asked Roger

"Plenty of evidence," replied Sergeant Jake, who suddenly stood up, "must go and find someone to nick," he added

'Nick' is a slang for 'arrest.' In this context.

With a cheesy smile he picked up his rag bag and walked out of the Café with a sluggish swagger.

Roger wondered how Jake was able to recognise him easily in a Café full of people even though he had changed his clothes. This time Roger was dressed in sartorial elegance: white shirt, black jacket and matching black trousers, a departure from his usual light blue donkey-jacket and tight jean-trousers which he had worn steadily for nearly one year. He had also grown a little beard. He felt secure in his new image, a disguise that was not intentionally conceived, nevertheless, he was quite happy with it. He picked up his newspaper and began to peruse again. Moments later, he proceeded to the counter and got another cup of coffee, while returning to his seat, he was shoved out of the way by a lady who had just rushed in to the Café and was speaking into her phone. As a result of the shove Roger's coffee spilt but the lady was nonchalant and oblivious to her action, she walked to the far side of the Café that was almost empty and sat down, still talking into her phone with full concentration. Roger was now irate, he went up to confront her. As he got nearer to her, lo and behold it was Charli, the lady who snatched Erika's hand-bag. He was frozen on the spot for the unexpected meeting with someone who had made negative newspaper headlines for causing misery to many innocent people, he was also overwhelmed to see Erika's hand bag which she placed on the seat beside her. He recognised the handbag because it was Erika's favourite which both he and Erika went out to purchase the previous Christmas period. However, since Charli did not pay any attention to Roger who had been standing beside her for a good two minutes, at which point he was able to confirm beyond reasonable doubt that it was her. Then he also realised that apart from seeing her in the restaurant when Erika alerted him to her and her companion during which they made a quick exit and escaped on a motorbike, he was also confident that he had somehow been associated with her sometime before. However, he was able to take note of the instructions she seemed to be giving to whoever that was at the other end of the phone. Instructions such as,

"Bring the motor bike in at exactly 4.30pm in the car park near the Airport beside a White Biggun car by the entrance, and don't be late"

She preened herself, put some lip-stick on and made a quick exit.

On Roger's watch it was 3.30pm. He hurried back to his seat, picked up his rock sack and the newspaper and went to the public phone booth and called the Inspector. To his disappointment he got a voice mail, so he left the following message.

"Expect my next call in the next five minutes, it is imperative that I speak to you."

Roger remained in the public phone booth glancing at his watch every few seconds. Impatiently, he dialled again two minutes later.

"Inspector Colin Smith," answered the Inspector

"Make sure you're at the car park near the Airport, beside a Biggun car which is parked at the entrance. Be there at 4.30pm. You will be certain to arrest the motorbike couple that had made headlines, the lady could be wearing jeans skirt and a revealing yellow blouse."

Before the Inspector could say anything or ask any questions, Roger replaced the receiver and left the public phone booth.

Again the Inspector began to pace back and forward in his office and then he stopped suddenly and looked at his watch and went into a deep thought after which he called in his team. By now he had no reason to doubt the mystery caller, on the contrary he was genuinely excited and was looking forward to another eventful day.

The Inspector quickly despatched two unmarked cars. In one of the cars were two detectives, one was hiding in the booth and the other was driving, while the second unmarked car was waiting just outside the car park driven by a detective. All had communication devices. At 4.10pm, the unmarked car with two detectives pulled into the car park near the Airport and was coasting to find an ideal parking space. However, they noticed a very expensive super car which was parked just at the entrance, the detectives concluded that the supper car could be their key word for a 'Biggun car.' At that time Charli had entered the car park and was loitering. She had been seen by the detectives and she fitted the description. Charli had also seen the detective's car but did not pay much attention as she was unaware it was an unmarked police car and she also noticed it was just one person in it, the driver. The car pulled into a space beside the supercar. The driver got out and walked off in full view of Charli. As far as she was aware, she was the only person in that part of the car park, unknown to her was the presence of a detective hiding in the booth.

It was around 4.25pm when a man on a motorbike entered the car park and went directly to where the supercar was parked and stopped. All this time, the detectives were communicating consistently and were ready for any eventuality. Little did they know that the plan would be changed at the last minute for they received an urgent instruction from the Inspector to follow the motorcyclist and Charli to their destination without blowing their cover.

At approximately 4.30pm, two men and a woman were dropped off by a taxi near the position of the super car, one of the men was carrying a brief case while the woman clutched what looked like a very expensive hand bag. They were just about to get in the super car when Charli walked up to them and asked if they could tell her the time. Then in a flash, she yanked the brief case from the man carrying it and turned to the woman, snatched her hand bag and jumped on to the motor bike and they sped away. The whole incident could have lasted five seconds. The man that was carrying the briefcase was astounded and he groaned in disbelief as he said to his companion whom he called 'Dee'

"It's the same woman,"

"What do you mean?" Dee asked

"The woman who took the briefcase from you last time," he replied

The unmarked car which was parked just outside the car park immediately tailed the couple on the motor bike to a five star hotel located about a mile from the Airport.

However, the Inspector was jubilantly milling around inside his office with great expectations, he had made an impact on his superiors for detaining the alleged Jewellery and file thieves and he was about to apprehend the motorbike-couple. His sudden success was creating waves within the home office and the Scotland Yard. The dismal price of a cup of coffee and a sandwich was beginning to positively change his fortune beyond his wildest dreams.

His reputation was significantly apparent as it began to spread day by day which in effect added some spring to his feeth. He was acutely aware that if he succeeded in nailing the motorbike couple, that he would not only keep his job but also climb greater heights within the police headquarters. His relationship with his superiors which were always coerced and often confrontational had suddenly began to take more positive accent and praise.

With his newly found positive outlook in life, he went back to his seat impatiently waiting for news from the detectives he had despatched to tail the motorbike couple from the airport carpark. He did not wait for long before he received a phone call informing him that the motorbike couple had been tailed to a hotel outside the airport.

"Do not let them out of your sight," he ordered

"Okay sir," said the detective

"I will send reinforcement, as soon as they arrive be sure to kick their door in, understand? He asked

"Yes sir, loud and clear," replied the detective

"Make sure their room is turned upside down, bring them to the station with whatever you can find, clear? He asked

"Clear sir," replied the detective

He swiftly despatched some reinforcement, invited the Press and paced his office for a while and sat down again in anticipation for some good news.

The reinforcement arrived at the hotel premises, they charged in to the couple's hotel room smashing the door down. Inside the room, the briefcase full of fifty pound notes was open and placed on the table. Some narcotics were littered on the bedside cabinet while Charli and her male companion laid stark naked in bed bewildered at the sudden invasion by the armed police who pointed guns at them. Detectives turned the room upside down and collected numerous forged bank cards, a lot of cash and some narcotics.

Swiftly, the couple were handcuffed and together with the seizures were taken to the police station where the Press had already gathered. The Inspector who was impatiently expecting good news was notified of their arrival. So, he left his office and quickly made his way to the station. On arrival he was escorted to the room where the culprits were kept and to his astonishment he came face to face with Charli his supposed fiancé in hand-cuffs. He was overwhelmed with disbelief. Definitely a jaw-dropping moment also for those who were present. The Inspector stood still frozen on the spot as he starred at Charli with a concoction of astonishment, hate and disgust. He took a couple of steps backwards and starred Charli in the eyes,

"This lady is supposed to be my fiancé,"

He swiftly left the room very disappointedly.

The Press went into total excitement and caused a pandemonium as they competed to get the best shots.

Consequently, from the epic of fulfilment the inspector was suddenly reduced to utter degradation.

CHAPTER 13

The following day, the news was splashed all over the national papers. Headline read, "Motorbike gang thieves captured: The Inspector's fiancé is one of them."

The arrest of the motorbike-couple soon spread like wild fire and the fact that Charli was supposedly the Inspector's fiancé was instrumental to the spread.

Roger was curiously anticipating to learn about the result of the information which he passed on to the Inspector. Since he relied on the free evening papers to satisfy his curiosity, he could not wait to get hold of one. He did not wait for long as the evening papers were usually littered at the train stations. Glancing over the shoulders a passenger who was perusing one of the papers, he could see the headline clearly but did not understand what it meant by 'The Inspector's fiancé is one of them.'

He got off at the next station, picked up the Evening paper and settled down next to one of the Kiosks on the platform to read the News with great interest. It was then that he realised that Charli, the woman who had caused a lot of mayhem, the woman who had snatched his girlfriend's hand bag was indeed the Inspector's fiancé and that they were about to get married. He was stunned when he read the News. As he reminisced, he remembered that the Inspector was with a woman the day he paid for his coffee and a sandwich on one of the station platforms, as the dust was beginning to clear he realised that the woman was indeed Charli. At that time, he was dressed appropriately which enabled her to camouflage her usual dress sense and made it immensely challenging for her to be recognised. He solved the puzzle by putting two and two together and sighed with relief.

Roger was beginning to question himself whether he did the right thing by being the catalyst for their arrest. Despite the fact that the Inspector's reputation had been on the ascent, nevertheless, he could now possibly be ridiculed because the woman he was about to wed was indeed a thief, a notorious thief.

Roger had one consolation, he was sure that Erika's hand bag would be recovered, that was the promise he made to Erika when they left the 'Rock on' restaurant. There were conflictions of thought in his mind for which he had no answer such as, 'was the Inspector aware of her negative tendencies. If he was, perhaps he thought she would abandon those tendencies when she became a police Inspector's fiancé, or was it simply due to her ability in concealing it from him when they met and thereafter. With all these wandering thoughts, Roger was indeed still none the wiser. To call the Inspector in order to get some answers crossed his mind and then he perished the thought and decided to call Erika instead, to give her the news that the lady who snatched her handbag had been arrested, which meant therefore, that reuniting with her handbag was surely imminent but for some reason he did not make the call.

Two months had passed and he had no contact with Erika or with his parents, so, he caught the next train to get to his usual public telephone box. He got there, then changed his mind and decided to use a different public call box instead should his location be traced.

He was quite knowledgeable about the locations of public phone boxes and made his way to another one. Finally he called Erika but received no joy, her telephone number did not exist anymore. Hoping that he had dialled a wrong number, he tried again and again but received the same response. He was head in hands for some time and despondently, he walked away quite confused. He immediately returned to the phone box and frantically called Marie, his mother who confirmed that Erika had not called her for quite some time, and had not told her if she had moved from her apartment or changed her phone number, in other words, she had no idea why her number had changed or terminated. Marie seized the opportunity to persuade him to return,

"When do you expect to come home?" Marie asked

"Mom, I still have a lot of work to accomplish," answered Roger

"Did you say work? What work?" asked Marie

"A lot of work mom," replied Roger

He hung up on her.

Roger perambulated on the platform for a time which seemed to him interminable which was due to the incomprehensibility of Erika's where-about or her circumstances, although several thoughts crossed his mind but none was convincingly positive. 'If only he could speak to Erika to let her know that her beloved handbag would soon be hanging down her shoulder again', he thought. Decidedly he went back to the public phone box and called the Inspector but he was unavailable, and that also added to his desperation. Finally, when all had failed, he called Julianna – for all intent and purposes she answered the phone with joyful vigour as usual,

"Hello, its Julianna here," She said

"Hi Julianna, this is Roger, do you remember me? Asked Roger

"How can I forget- Roger, where have you been? She enquired

"Listen, can I come round now?" He asked

"Of course you can," she answered

Roger soon was on his way to Julianna's. Suddenly, it dawned on him that her house had become a cocoon of solace and a joyful and vibrant base in which to energise himself. He remembered vividly how during his penultimate visit to her penthouse when there were a lot of people, he was received with open arms despite the fact that he did not know anyone there except Julianna whom he had only met ones before, yet he felt amazingly and completely at home. Then his thought shifted to the general ambiance of the penthouse in retrospect, the view across the bridge from the balcony, the river Thames flowing in all its majesty within the surrounds and the sporadic little speed boats cruising as if they were gently caressing the serene surface of the river. He felt it was indeed the longest journey he would ever make, he was looking forward to getting there to see Julianna again after recent events that had taken place in quick successions in which he was undoubtedly consumed with mixed feelings, particularly with Erika's unexpected and sudden disappearance or silence. Whichever it was, she certainly had succeeded in playing perhaps - mind game with him, to his detriment.

He was truly delighted when he finally got off the train at Vauxhall station. He was aware that in a matter of minutes he would be pressing Julianna's buzzer to be let in. Eventually he was in the lift and then he pressed the buzzer,

"Is that you Roger?" asked Julianna,

"Yes," he answered

"Come right up," she said

As soon as he entered the penthouse he was warmly welcomed by her, instead of settling in the lounge, he walked past, brushing her aside and proceeded directly to the balcony for the awesome view. She followed him,

"Feeling peckish?" she asked

"How could you tell?" he asked

"I am starving, so I guessed you were too," she said

"You guessed correctly, I could eat a horse right now, including the rider," he said

Julianna chuckled,

"How is your friend Soisin?" he asked

"She is fine I guess, I have not seen her for a long while, she is now sharing a pad with another girl around Chiswick in West London," she replied

"Friend of hers?" he asked

"I guess so, they met in a Supermarket and since then, they have not been apart," replied Julianna

Julianna left Roger abruptly on the balcony and went into the kitchen while Roger continued to admire the view with overwhelming fascination. In no time at-all, Julianna had prepared some delightful dishes and laid them on the dining table with a good bottle of red wine thrown in. She filled two glasses with wine and took them to the balcony where Roger was still fascinated with the extraordinary scenery of the river Thames and the activities within it, also, the view across the bridge which accessed the city of London's skyline. She handed him a glass of wine and invited him over to the dining table. He took the glass of wine and followed her.

Roger was astounded when he saw the table adorned with sumptuous cuisine and a large bowl of salad, including a vintage bottle of red wine. He tucked in straight away with great appetite.

"Have you had Buddhist discussion meeting after the one that I attended?" he asked

"Yes, many, we have regular meetings," she replied

He gazed at her sternly,

"Have you achieved absolute happiness?" He asked

"Any particular reason for asking?" she asked

"Since it is one of the benefits of the practice, I wondered if you had," he paused, "you seem to be subliminally happy and generous, believe me it shows, so, one wonders if it was an attribute of the practice," he added

"Thank you for your compliment, however, it is every one's right to be happy and by chanting the one essential phrase which is, Nam-Myo-Ho-Renge-Kyo, one is guaranteed absolute happiness and a fulfilling life by taking actions to fulfil it irrespective of one's circumstances," she said

"Did you say 'guaranteed?" he asked

"Yes, definitely," she confidently replied, "not only that, one will also find True self, Eternity, Happiness and Purity which are really one's true virtues, however, to answer your first question which was, 'have I achieved absolute happiness,' the answer to that is that - absolute happiness is not a destination that one reaches and says 'yes, I have reached it and that's it, but by continually practising and chanting the one essential phrase, one is able to sustain and strengthens one's resolve to win in life, no matter what life may throw in one's path, therefore, absolute happiness or true happiness is in fact having the tool to take on each huddle, overcome it, and become wiser and stronger in the process"

After they had the sumptuous meal, they resigned to the lounge each with a glass of wine. The television was on the News channel with the News that the motorbike-couple had been tried in the court and found guilty also that the Jewellery thieves had been found guilty, also that the woman who trolled journalists and politicians with blackmail was indeed Charli as well. The News also mentioned that the brave Inspector who masterminded their arrest was at large, that no-one knew of his where-about after he discovered that his fiancé was indeed the notorious culprit. Roger was glued to the television with acute concentration that Julianna became curious and asked,

"You are absorbed by the news, what was it all about?"

Obviously, he did not wish to blow his cover by admitting he was the architect of the entire episode or that he knew anything about it.

"Just glad they've been caught, they made people's lives unbearable," he replied

"I know someone whose bag was snatched by that woman, what is her name ...."

As she was trying to recall her name,

"Do you mean Charli?" he asked

"That's right, that was her name – 'Charli', she replied

"She snatched a young lady's precious hand bag just near my favourite restaurant and escaped on a motor bike with her accomplice," he said

"It is a puzzle that the Inspector disappeared," she said

"That's my real concern," he said

They spent most of the day discussing the hunt of the delinquents and their eventual capture while they sipped their glass of wine.

Roger was surprised but pleased that Julianna had not asked him where he lived or what he did for work and still invited him to her penthouse alone to partake in a sumptuous meal. He wondered whether she would ever want to know more of him. Nevertheless, he knew that it was perilous for a beautiful young lady to invite a total stranger in her home alone. 'Could she be that trusting that she was so gullible not to think of the dangers that might entail,' he thought.

Julianna was quite relaxed and nonchalant, she left him in the lounge and entered the kitchen. Roger was thinking if she had broken off with her boyfriend or whether she had had any boyfriend at-all. Julianna has such a warm and cheerful personality and with astounding beauty to go with it, coupled with the fact that she was also a great cook. Suddenly, she reappeared from the kitchen,

"I have put the kettle on, fancy a coffee?" She asked

As she stood in front of Roger with a smile that could melt an ice-cube instantly, Roger was lost for words as he glanced at her silky orange dress that revealed the silhouette of her elegant slim body, showing her flawless curves. She knew quite well that he was captivated, as she waited for a reply. Eventually, he ecstatically replied with a grin,

"Would love a cup of coffee, thank you,"

Julianna chuckled and re-entered the kitchen. Moments later- she re-joined Roger in the lounge, carrying a small tray containing variety of biscuits, chocolates and two cups of coffee.

Late in the evening, Julianna was ready to do her evening Buddhist practice, so she asked him to join her to which he gladly accepted. They recited the sutra and chanted Nam-myoho-renge-kyo for a considerable length of time.

At the end of the chant, he was ready to depart and he turned round and gazed at her thoughtfully,

"Can I ask you a question?

"Please do," she replied

"Why did you chuckle when I told you I would like to have coffee?" he asked

"Because your thought was loud, I could hear it," she replied, "you fancied me did you not?"

The tone of her reply was rather astonishing and spell bounding to Roger, he did not expect her not to mince her words, but he knew she was right.

"Why is it that most of the time men could not read the minds of women?" he asked

"But women can easily read the minds of men, it's not rocket science," she giggled

"You have certainly proved it," he said

She gave Roger a friendly peck on the chick and asked him to sit down. She dialled a taxi to pick him up but he declined and insisted he would prefer to find his way instead but she insisted adding that the taxi was already on its way. Few minutes later she looked out of the window and informed him that the Taxi had arrived and stuffed a fifty pound note inside his top pocket.

He entered the lift and boarded the taxi. The driver was surprised when Roger told him that his destination was Vauxhall train station which was only about a hundred metres away. Obviously, Julianna had no idea where he lived and did not want to make him uncomfortable if he did not want to disclose his address, but she was aware that the fifty pound note would be enough for a drop to any address within London from Vauxhall.

CHAPTER 14

However, the taxi turned a corner and stopped at the traffic light and suddenly a stretched limousine pulled up beside the taxi and two women jumped out, the stretched limousine drove off swiftly. The women forced the taxi's door open and got in, both women pulled out short guns from their respective hand bags and ordered the taxi driver to drive on. When they had crossed a bridge, he was ordered to pull over in front of a stretched limousine which was packed by the roadside. Roger had noticed it was the same limousine from which the women got out at the traffic light, he also realized it was a hijack but could not fathom why. He began to chant 'Nam-myo-h0-renge-kyo' inaudibly so he could be protected in the ominous situation that he was in. He had read in one of the books given to him by Julianna which says that 'when Buddhahood is manifested from within, it gains protection from without'.

Roger and the taxi driver were forced into the stretched limousine accompanied by the two women still holding their short guns against the back of their heads. Roger was aware that the driver of the limousine was also a woman who also had a short gun placed on the driver's seat between her thighs. The windows were tinted so, neither the taxi driver nor Roger could identify their location on that unexpected journey. However, after some interminable fifty minutes they were driven through a large gate onto the grounds of an imposing large house and stopped. There, they were taken to a very small room at the back of the house. It was only Roger and the taxi driver in this room, he started chanting but this time audibly. The taxi driver gazed at him solemnly,

'What is that about?"

"If you join me in this chant, there is a good chance we can come out of this unscathed," Roger replied with a smile, "I will explain later."

The taxi driver ignored Roger's invitation to chant with him, however he later joined him but with reluctance. In the small room, there was a single bed in the corner and a table at the far side by the window and two chairs. A red hand bag was on the table by the window which was placed there accidentally by one of the women that brought them in.

Then suddenly there was argument by the two women and a couple of men who were in the other room which was separated by just a wall with the small room were Roger and the taxi driver were kept. The women's voices and that of the two men could be heard very clearly by Roger and the taxi driver because what they were saying were coming out of the radio inside the red hand bag. Roger went close to the bag to check if it contained a gun, wondering whether the woman who accidentally left the hand bag on that table had perhaps forgotten to remove her gun from it. On close examination, the red hand bag only contained a make-up kit, a diary, and a radio communication device.

Roger swiftly perused the diary page by page, contrary to his expectation the taxi driver was astonishingly infuriated that Roger looked through the diary. He asked Roger to switch off the radio.

"What is your name buddy?" Roger asked

"Jim," replied the taxi driver

"Jim, why do you want me to switch off the radio?" Roger asked

"Because if they knew we heard all they said, we could get into a lot of trouble and we may be lynched," replied Jim

"We are already in a lot of trouble," Roger said, "the only wise thing to do now is to find a way and get out of it,"

"Wouldn't the chant do it as you said?" asked Jim

"Yes, chant so you will take the right action," replied Roger

Then came a very loud knock from the inside of the garage which was at the back of the house, the loud knock prompted Roger and the taxi driver to momentarily keep quiet but the knock persisted and louder, developing into what seemed like an intentional act of desperation and despondency. Roger eavesdropped to perceive what sounded like a cry for help emanating from the inside of the garage. What surprised Roger was that Jim did not seem to be concerned with what sounded like a cry for help and the continuous banging from the garage, he was rather unperturbed.

Form the radio in the red hand bag, what started like an argument had developed into a full scale row and there was a pandemonium.

Through the window of the small room, Roger could see two other women running out from the door at the side of the house towards the gate, they were being chased by the women who at gun- point, had just brought Roger and Jim to the house. Throughout the commotion Jim could not bat an eyelid, he was relaxed and oblivious. At this point what Roger had heard from the radio in the red hand bag was literarily unfolding before his eyes. The realisation was that while the two women were out, their husbands had invited their mistresses in for sex and were caught red handed by their wives. Roger was terrified when one of the women, obviously disgruntled, stormed into their small room with rage, held the door ajar and asked him and the taxi driver to leave. Roger, though without hesitation but certainly gobsmacked made a quick exit and ran toward the gate. When he had passed the gate, he looked back for Jim who was lagging behind, he was a little confused to see him apparently having a friendly chat with the woman who had opened their door and told them to leave. He was not in a hurry to get in his taxi which was still where he left it earlier. However, Roger took to his heels until he had left the expansive grounds of the house to the main road where he flagged down a lift.

CHAPTER 15

It was in the early hours of the following morning that he arrived in front of a train station to find there were no services, the station had closed. As there was nowhere for him to get some sleep or to rest, he wandered around in the streets for a while chanting Nam-myoho-renge-kyo. As he turned a corner into a narrow street, he was relieved to find a night-club still open, it was very busy. Couples were going to and from the club hand-in-hand, kissing and laughing. Feeling very cold and tired, he stood across the road opposite the night club watching all the goings-on, retrospectively the pleasant memories of how he and Erika used to frequent night clubs flooded his tired mind.

Then he realised that he still got the fifty pound note which Julianna forced into his pocket for his taxi fare, he decided he would go into the club. He did not have any other option since the train station was closed and he had been running to get away from the house where he was held captive with Jim. He was now very tired and conflicting thoughts possessed his already tired mind. Even if he could only sit down and get some rest till the train station opened, that would be sufficient enough to get his energy back. So, he crossed the road, paid the entry fee at the door and got in.

The club was at its element, music was blaring, the dance floor was full, and lighting was colourful and energetic. It was truly an exciting environment. He walked quietly to the back corner and sat down. Though he was resisting to fall asleep but the electrifying ambiance helped to keep him awake. Suddenly his eyes caught the sight of a girl leaving the dance floor, she was in the company of two men. He sat up, rubbed his weak eyes as if to rejuvenate them and then gazed again intently. The girl was of the same height, same way of walking and had almost the same dress sense as his fiancé Erika, she also had the same handbag but in a different colour and similar mannerisms as her. Roger immediately stood up and stormed on to the dance floor yelling 'Erika! Erika!

Pushing through everyone on his path as he chased after the girl he was still yelling 'Erika! At this time all activities within the club came to a gridding halt, all eyes were now on him.

Eventually, he caught up with the girl and the two men at the exit. Standing very close to her he was overly disappointed, she was not Erika. He was dejected and truly frustrated, he turned round and staggered back into the club.

From that moment, he could not get rid of the thought of Erika from his mind. However, occasionally he would revert to thinking of the knocks and banging from the inside of the garage at the house in which he was confined with Jim. He was acutely aware that there were people inside that garage, he heard a voice crying for help, he wondered why he and Jim were kidnapped at gun point and also of the fate of those inside the garage crying for help. The thought that mystified him the most was certainly why Jim did not panic throughout their captivity and also why he had time to relax and chat to the woman when she stormed into their small room, it was an action typical of a woman scorned.

At about 04.00am that morning, the crowd began to disperse from the club, so he made his way to the train station which was quite a long work from the club but when he got there, it was still not open which meant that services were unavailable. He wandered around for another hour, by the time he returned, the station was open and services resumed. He had done a lot of walking since he was kidnapped and his stomach was empty, consequently his energy was trifling rapidly.

Roger caught a train and made his way directly to his favourite station café, the same Café where he saw Charli talking on the phone to her accomplice. There, he had a full plate of breakfast and settled down to read the free news-paper he had picked up on his way. He was surprised and displeased that there was no news about Inspector Colin Smith. He put the news-paper aside and reminisced about the principles of Buddhism. 'Could chanting Nam-myoho-renge-kyo in that small room be the reason for their unexpected release,' he questioned himself, 'if so what about those locked up in the garage crying for help'.

He furiously went to the phone box and called the Inspector's mobile number, he was not expecting to get an answer but was pleasantly surprised when a voice came through,

"Inspector Smith here," answered the Inspector

"Glad to hear your voice again, Inspector," said Roger

"Who is this," asked the Inspector

"Same person that gave you information that led to the arrest of the motor-bike couple and the Jewellery thieves," replied Roger

"That's fine, could you tell me what your name was or where you are?" asked the Inspector

"Never mind that, how are you getting on with the Victoria station case?" Roger asked

"No development on that yet, so, it's been put on hold," replied the Inspector

"Okay then, I have another case for you', very urgent, got to be done now," insisted Roger

The Inspector fell silent,

"There is a very imposing and gated house a few miles before Oxfordshire, turn off from the motorway M-1153. Past the farm house on the left, you'll find it to your right, you can't miss it. Perhaps you'll see a stretched limousine parked on the forecourt,"

"So what's up there?" the Inspector asked

"When you get there, head straight to the garage at the back," continued Roger, "I believe some people are locked up in there, most likely kidnapped."

"Will be done right away," said the Inspector

"You've to get there fast," said Roger

"Can you tell me your name?" the Inspector asked

"Eyeball," replied Roger

Roger hung up

Although the Inspector had not gone back to the police HQ after arresting his fiancé Charli and her accomplice was still giving orders through his phone. It crossed his mind that this person who called himself 'Eyeball' had played a major part in re-instating his credibility in the police force. Also 'Eyeball' had become a strong and reliable instrument for taking many criminals out of the streets. He owed him a lot and would like to at least meet up with him. The Inspector had taken all the credits for successfully arresting and prosecuting the delinquents but the person behind all the success remained behind the scene and virtually incognito.

Roger's mind was occupied with the thought of Erika, and then slowly shifted to his aging parents. He understood that his father, Mr Dean worked very hard which meant that his mother remained alone at home. What had happened to Erika was his primary unanswered question, he noted that whatever caused her disappearance would be very serious indeed because not even his mother Marie, could have an answer to that despite the fact that they'd often conferred with each other since Roger left home. So, he decided to try her phone again in the hope that if it had been faulty before, it would have been rectified by now. He called Erika's number from his mobile phone but to no avail. It still had a disconnected tone. He then called his mother but there was no answer. He found a bench at the station and sat down head in hand.

After chanting Nam-Myoho-Renge-kyo for some minutes he walked straight toward the exit. He was determined to get to Erika's apartment and find out by himself what had occurred. With the Buddhist spirit of resilience he was determined not to be defeated in reuniting with his childhood love and was also determined to see his dear mother whom he had abandoned for over one year. Buddhism has instilled a sense of compassion and humanity and responsibility into his seemingly warped state. The popular saying that 'you'll never appreciate what you have until you lose it,' strongly epitomised in his being. It was simply karma transforming into mission.

He arrived at Erika's apartment and pressed the doorbell a few times but there was no response. Then he noticed the blinds and curtains were drawn, the lounge was dark and he could not see through even though it was day time. Standing by the front door thinking of the next step to take, he noticed a neighbour's curtains twitching. He walked across and rang the neighbour's doorbell, a lady came out and confirmed that Erika had moved out of the apartment six weeks earlier. Roger could not contain his terrible sense of loss and frustration, tears rolled down his cheeks. The lady, bewildered by his sorrowful countenance, could not help but invited him in for a cup of tea to which he humbly declined.

"Any idea where she moved to?" he asked

"No, I saw a removal van taking her things and when I asked her, she simply told me she was moving out," replied the lady

Disappointedly, Roger decided to follow up some leads such as her favourite supermarket, hairdresser, bank, and the nearest train station, He thought if he waited in front of the station that there could be a possibility of seeing her either going in or coming out of the station. Same possibility applied for her hair dresser, bank and super-market.

He spent the following couple of weeks trudging from the station to supermarket and the bank in the hope of finding her but there was no sign of her. His determination to find her was swiftly becoming dismal but had not completely waned, so he called his mother on the phone and yet there was no response. He hailed a taxi and made his way to his parents' house, on arrival to the front of the house, he noticed that neither his mum's nor his father's car was in the drive. So he knocked on the front door but there was no response. Only then that he realised that he had arrived to an empty house. The flower pot hanging by the front door was not there anymore and part of the drive had been paved, curtains changed with new fabric, new double glazing had also been installed. These were a few changes that had taken place since his departure. Then he began to wonder if his parents had also moved out.

CHAPTER 16

Roger was relieved when he turned his key in the front door and it opened without difficulty, only then he became convinced that it was actually the same house, his parents' house. He got in the lounge to find every furniture still in the same place and none had been changed, then slowly he entered his room and stood there for a while examining every nook and cranny but there was no change. The only visible changes that were discernible of course were cleanliness and orderliness because his mother Marie, cleaned his room almost daily and folded his clothes which were previously scattered all over his bed. She had got used to the routine that she cleaned and tidied it whether it was already clean or tidy. Roger sat on his bed consumed in thought. He felt so lonely and the house was so quiet that one could hear a pin drop.

Roger could not comprehend how all that was dear to him was disappearing before his eyes or literarily changed to his detriment in a little over a year. He was so confused and terrified that he could not envisage asking the neighbours or contacting any of his relatives to find out the where-about of his parents. He was fraught with contentious presumptions of un-imaginable proportions: firstly, Erika had left her apartment and did not leave any clue where she had moved to, and also his parents had astrangely deserted the house. He wondered if it was a plan hatched to get their own back at him. The more he thought of all these, the more none the wiser he became.

It was late at night and he was getting hungry, so he switched all the lights on and opened the fridge and was pleased to find it was well stocked. He fried up some bacons, opened a can of baked beans, toasted slices of bread and settled down to eat when suddenly, he could hear some commotion outside and then came a voice from the loud speaker,

"This is the police, come out with both your hands on your head" said the police

Roger was terrified, he went closer to the window and peered outside, and was amazed to see several police cars parked in front of the house and the police marks men took positions with their guns, using the police cars as shields. Another voice came on the loudspeaker.

"This is the police, come out slowly with both your hands on your head!"

Roger panicked and thought the game was up, that the police had finally found out he was responsible for the Victoria station incident. At that moment he was unsure of what to do, and kept perambulating from the lounge to the kitchen hoping to find a solution to this quandary. However, as he looked through the kitchen window at the back, he noticed that the house was also surrounded by the police.

Roger honestly wished he had stayed on the trains were he was quite independent, free and created value by helping to keep criminals off the street. He had only left the train for a day and his world was collapsing on him, all because he came out to look for Erika. He had no option but to come out as he was instructed by the police. Walking to the front door slowly he opened the door and with both his hands on his head, he came out the front and was immediately hand-cuffed and forced into a police van and whisked off to a local police station.

At the police station Rogen learned that the reason for his arrest was that he was suspected of burglary. Apparently someone had reported to the police that a dangerous intruder was in his house. When Roger told the police that he lived in the house, they were puzzled. Nevertheless, Mr Dean, Roger's father, was immediately contacted by the police to identify and untangle the tapestry. However, Roger was pleased to know that his arrest had nothing to do with the Victoria station incident. The police was not even aware that he was the person responsible for it. Mr Dean, Roger's father arrived at the police station a few minutes' later and was escorted to the cell where Roger was kept. On entry, Mr Dean was speechless as he came face to face with Roger, he was frozen and his feelings were mixed. On one hand, he was pleased to see his son after one year, on the other hand, he was not excited that Roger returned home in such a way that aroused suspicion and fear amongst his neighbours by involving the police.

It played out that Roger's parents returned very late at night, as they drove to the front of the house, were terrified to see the lights on, and a shadow loitering inside and assumed it was a very dangerous person, as it was on the news a few days earlier that a convicted murderer had escaped from prison. However, Roger was released and followed his father home. A couple of police officers who remained at Mr Dean's house to guard it pending investigation and to look after Marie while Mr Dean responded to the police call to identify Roger. At the police station they were also awestruck to learn that the suspected criminal was indeed Mr Dean's son. Some of the officers some-how were ashamed of the silliness of the entire police activity earlier and went back to the station silently deflated.

Late at night that day after the police had dispersed from Mr Dean's house, Roger had gone in to his room while his parents remained in the lounge, hardly any word from Marie or Mr Dean as they sat quietly reminiscing of the events earlier that night, they had decided to leave Roger alone till morning. However, Marie prepared some salad and a rump-steak and took it on a plate to Roger's room and placed it on the table but he was just sitting on his bed gazing into nothingness. She closed the door behind her and left the room. The following morning, Marie had set up some breakfast on the table and sat with Mr Dean over coffee and slices of toast and waited for Roger to join them. Roger did not join them for breakfast, so, Mr Dean stood up with rage and began to walk towards Roger's room for eventual rebuke,

"Where do you think you are going?" She asked

"Where do you think I'm going?" asked Mr Dean in reply

"Just be gentle with him, will you," said Marie, "remember, over a year ago, I walked into that room when he did not turn up for breakfast and he was not there, so please be gentle with him," pleaded Marie

"This time I am going to drag him out," said Mr Dean

"Do not let history repeat itself," said Marie calmly

Mr Dean stormed off to Roger's room and opened the door but Roger was not there. He stood still for a while and turned back making his way back to the breakfast table dazed and speechless. Marie noticed that his belligerent behaviour had rapidly subdued and reduced to a feeling of helplessness and disdain,

"So, what happened?" asked Marie

"The bloody fool has gone again!" he yelled

Marie fell silent and deep in thought while Mr Dean plunked himself in the settee in utter hopelessness. Neither of them had any appetite for breakfast anymore, so the breakfast remained on the dining table untouched. Silence descended upon the household again. Later on in the evening of that day, Mr Dean and Marie were considering reporting to the police but realised it would be to their ridicule because Roger was not under age, he was a grown up and an independent adult coupled with the fact that they had had enough of police activity at the house lately and were not in the mood for concerning the police with their family challenges.

Late at night, Mr Dean and Marie had just settled down as it had been their daily routine to watch the daily news on TV when the front door opened and Roger staggered in. His parents glanced at him with due astonishment but did not utter a word to him. He went directly to the dining table which was still adorned with the now cold breakfast. It had not been removed since they discovered that Roger had disappeared once again that morning. Without much ado, he began to gulp down the breakfast in large portions. Marie noticed that the manner in which Roger was guzzling the food was a sure sign of starvation. Marie, therefore, walked into the kitchen to prepare hot dinner for him when Mr Dean confronted her in the kitchen and gave her a sign indication that she should not bother preparing any food for him. They both re-entered the lounge and continued watching the News, intentionally oblivious to Roger's presence.

Within a short space of time Roger had cleaned off the entire breakfast, poured himself a cup of coffee and joined his parents to watch the News. Still there was no conversation between them. His parents went to bed at midnight while he stayed up trying to figure out how and where to find Erika.

Four nights in a row, Roger did not join his parents for breakfast and had not discussed anything with them, he had been leaving the house very early each morning and returning late at night. His parents had decided not to prompt him to talk to them until he wished to, for that reason they ceased to check up for him in the morning. Mr

Dean was gradually losing his patience for Roger's behaviour which he considered grossly inappropriate.

One early morning, Roger came out of his room and proceeded to the lounge in order to exit through the front door. He unexpectedly saw Mr Dean waiting to confront him in the lounge,

"Where do you think you're going?" asked Mr Dean

"Out," Roger replied

"You are not going anywhere," said Mr Dean, as he stood between Roger and the front door. Roger tried to shove past but Mr Dean stood his ground.

"You have to join your mum and I for breakfast today, but if you decide to go out instead, make sure you do not come back to this house." Said Mr Dean.

Mr Dean walked back to his bedroom.

Roger stood still for a few minutes, turned back and went back to his room. Later that morning, Marie prepared breakfast as usual and sat by the table with Mr Dean eating the breakfast and contrary to their expectation, Roger sluggishly appeared at the table and joined them. The silence was almost exhausting to Marie, she could not hold it any longer, so, she stared at Roger momentarily,

"Your father and I are wondering if you are well, son." Said Marie softly,

"I am very well, mom," Roger reluctantly replied

"He looks well, it is his attitude that is grossly sickening," said Mr Dean

"Stop it!" Marie exclaimed

Roger gazed at his mother solemnly, pleased that she reprimanded his father

"I am alright mom," said Roger sheepishly

"So where have you been going to every morning since you returned home a few days ago?" Marie asked compassionately

"Searching for Erika," he replied

"Good to know that love still rules, she did not stop pinning for you when you were away," Marie said measuredly

"You completely ignored your parents who did not see you for over a year, but you have the time to look for Erika," his father interrupted

"Ignore him Roger, your father has no clue about the power of that word called love," said Marie sarcastically

"Do you realise you are spoiling him, he is a grown man," said Mr Dean

"He is still my little boy, whether he is a grown man or a child," she replied

After breakfast, Roger went out straight from the breakfast table. Marie and Mr Dean were hopeful that he was making some progress, at least he had started talking which was delightfully preferable to the usual sort of silence that had prevailed.

CHAPTER 17

Erika had begun to wonder whether her ploy to move out of her apartment would have any positive effect on her relationship with Roger. After-all Erika's reason for moving was necessitated by the fact that Roger had neglected her for over one year and the only time she saw him during that period was when they had a meal at the restaurant together, the day her hand bag was snatched by Charli and her accomplice. She devised the ploy with a view to ascertaining if Roger would miss her and try to find her. The truth was that she was still madly in love with him but was unsure if he would reciprocate the love. She was tired and traumatized for being without him and did not know where he was or what he did since he disappeared from his parents' house.

Though, faced with these uncertainties, she was still irrepressible to finding out the truth. Frequently, she visited their favourite restaurant alone in the hope of finding him. It had crossed her mind to call Marie but that would defeat the purpose of her ploy, so, she perished the thought in the belief that if he yearned for her like she did him, the probability would be that Roger would discard his apparent selfishness and look for her and she was determined to make him do that. With these conflicting thoughts, unknown to her was that Roger had returned home and was fervently looking for her to the extent that it had caused a rift between himself and his parents.

Based on instinct rather than reality or high probability which was indicative of some-one stressed and confused, she decided to proceed to Sloan square tube station to look for him owing to the simple fact that it was the nearest tube station to their favourite restaurant. It was a mystery that as she walked down the stairs on to the platform, the doors of the train which was already on the platform closed. She could see Roger through the window as the train was about to leave and she screamed 'Roger!' but the train pulled away. Tears rolled down her cheeks uncontrollably. She'd just missed him by a couple of seconds, unfortunately Roger did not see her, he continued on his way to Victoria station to look around for her.

From that day on, Erika went to Sloane square tube station every day for one week, she would stand on the platform at exactly the same spot from where she saw Roger previously in the hope that she would see him again, but to no avail.

On her last day at Sloane square tube station, she accidentally met Julianna going home from shopping. Julianna who had not seen Erika for about two weeks since she was introduced to her by Soisin as her new apartment mate, was surprised to observe that Erika had strangely emaciated within a short period of time. Julianna invited Erika for coffee at the Café just outside the station with the intention of finding out from her why she had lost a lot of weight. As soon as they settled down at the Café, Julianna could not hold back her curiosity any longer,

"You have lost a lot of weight," said Julianna

"Loss of appetite for food caused it," Erika replied

"Why did you lose appetite?" Julianna asked

"Going through difficult time at the moment," she replied

Julianna assumed the difficulty was as a result of social economic classism because she had heard from Soisin that Erika had not only moved out from her previous apartment but also had left her job at the same time in order to get away completely from the locality. However, contrary to her assumption, Erika's difficulties had nothing to do with pecuniary reasons but simply that it was due to prolonged none communication or contact with Roger, and therefore felt neglected by him for over a year. Erika had not told Soisin and Julianna about the love of her life and neither did they know that Roger whom they had met before had any connection with Erika.

Roger returned home one evening after searching for Erika, he was drenched in the rain while his parents sat comfortably in the lounge watching the evening News on the television. He walked in and went straight to his room to dry up, Marie and Mr Dean glanced at each other and raised their eye-brows but not a single word to Roger. Few minutes' later Roger appeared in the lounge and joined them. Marie looked at him compassionately,

"Food is in the kitchen, help yourself," said Marie

"I am not hungry mom, there is no appetite," replied Roger

"It is about Erika, is it not?" enquired Marie

"Yes," he replied

"I did not think it was in her character to disappear like that and not let any-one know, but you did exactly the same to everyone," said Marie

Mr Dean was getting agitated listening to Marie and Roger's conversation,

"Now you know how it feels, do you expect her just to sit down and wait for you? Life goes on, with or without you," said Mr Dean.

The conversation was halted when the breaking news appeared with the headline:

"The most dangerous International gang was busted today with the help of someone who called himself 'Eyeball'."

At this point, Roger was particularly glued to the TV.

The news was that the gang, an international syndicate was responsible for the kidnapping and smuggling of people across international boundaries, the gang, a sophisticated network of international criminal organisation was also involved in money laundering which the law enforcement was aware of but unable to apprehend the criminals due to lack of evidence which would be used in prosecution. The news also stated that seven people including three children were rescued from a locked garage.

The Inspector apparently felt some guilt for taking the credit of the previous arrests which were facilitated with the information provided by Roger, he was overwhelmingly astonished by the accuracy and reliability of his information that he had decided to mention his name 'Eyeball' which was Roger's assumed name. Roger's parents also shared strong interest in the news. Mr Dean wondered whether the person called 'Eyeball' was a disgruntled criminal member that he was able to give the police the information which led to the arrest of the gang.

A few days later, Roger boarded a train in his usual quest to find Erika. When he picked up a free evening paper he was petrified to see the picture of Jim, the taxi driver with whom he was kidnapped, his jaws dropped as he held the paper in his trembling hands. He read the article that followed to discover that Jim was indeed a member of the gang. In retrospect, the penny dropped as to why Jim was nonchalant the whole time they were locked up in the small room and why he had told him to switch of the radio device in the red handbag that was placed on the table near the window. Lastly, as to why after the lady had opened the door with rage and asked him and Jim to leave, Jim still stayed back to chat with her, the jigsaw was beginning to fit.

Roger returned home and joined his parent to watch the news, It was the same news about the International criminal syndicate that monopolise the news bulletin that week.

Mr Dean and Marie were fascinated with the news, Again Mr Dean said that 'Eyeball' could be a disgruntled member of the gang because the information given by Eyeball to the police was incredibly accurate. Nevertheless he also strongly praised 'Eyeball' irrespective of whether he was a disgruntled member of the gang or not. Roger could not bear to keep quiet so, he intervened,

"How could you say that, Dad," interrupted Roger

"What do you mean?" Mr Dean asked

"That 'Eyeball' was a disenchanted member of the gang," replied Roger, "It was his mission to give the information that led to the arrest of the gang, to expose and defeat evil. Eyeball's information was to stop others from suffering and also to stop the culprits making more bad causes that were steeped in greed, – do you not think, cause and effect is very strict and impartial," Roger explained

Mr Dean was suddenly speechless at the strong words from Roger coupled with the fact that it was the first time he had spoken to him since his return Marie was also perplexed.

They wondered where Roger got his bright philosophy from. However, the thought of Erika, and her handbag were still in his mind, he had promised her he would recover her cherished handbag and therefore he decided to contact the Inspector to enquire about it.

CHAPTER 18

The Inspector had returned to his office and had settled down for over a month, consequently for his apparent monumental endeavours in successfully clearing his case files he had been promoted to the post of Commissioner. While sitting in his new office, not a single day had past that he did not think of Eyeball in the knowledge that neither he nor his officers could have been able to solve any of the cases that were assigned to him. They did not have the faintest idea of where to start. The worst case scenario would have been to lose his job long before that. So, he wished he could one day meet up with Eyeball to pay his debt of gratitude. However, one thing that still stuck in his mind was the circumstances surrounding the brief case or rather two briefcases.

One month had past and no-one had reported losing a briefcase full of money, this however aroused suspicion within the police department. The Inspector internalised the fact that it was definitely another case he had to resolve excluding the Victoria station incident case which had gone cold. If he had been on duty at the time when Roger returned home and Mr Dean's house was surrounded by police officers, he could have brought him in for an aggressive questioning but due to circumstances surrounding the arrest of his fiancé Charli he was away and not in the office at the time therefore, he was ignorant of the incident.

On the following day, Roger had gone out yet again in search of Erika but the search remained futile so, he collected a couple of free daily newspapers and went to the usual Café at the train station to peruse the daily news. He was excited to read about the invisible 'Eyeball' and how the Commissioner wished they could meet face to face. Roger felt an acute sense of achievement in divulging the information which led to the eventual arrest of the criminals, saving the Inspector Colin Smith's job and also for being a catalyst in his promotion to Commissioner. He became engrossed in the delight of knowing he had successfully accomplished his mission or had he. Then his mind reverted to thinking of Erika which at that moment was the mission he would very much like to accomplish which was to be reunited with her.

He went to the usual phone box, as he began to dial he wondered if the previous Inspector's number had been changed now he had become the Commissioner, nevertheless he dialled the usual number,

"Hello, Commissioner speaking," came the voice

Roger was unsure if it was him, after-all it had been a considerable time lapse since their last communication. He decided to ask for the Inspector as he previously had done.

"Is Inspector Colin Smith available," Roger enquired

"Commissioner Colin Smith speaking," replied the voice

Roger was now certain he was speaking to the right person.

"Congratulations on your new responsibility," said Roger

"Thank you, may I know who is speaking? Ask the Commissioner

"Eyeball, remember me?" asked Roger

"How can I forget?" replied the Commissioner "You've been most helpful and your strong tips were monumentally effective, now that I am the Commissioner therefore, in a strong position to compensate you, I really wish we could meet up – anytime and anywhere of your choice"

"To compensate me," asked Roger

"Yes, in the form of benefit for your outstanding work," replied the Commissioner.

"Do you realise there are different kinds of benefit?" Roger asked

"What exactly do you mean," he asked

"My mentor, Daisaku Ikeda explains there are two kinds of benefits that arise from faith in the Mystic Law: Conspicuous and Inconspicuous. Conspicuous benefit is the obvious, visible benefit of being protected or being quickly able to surmount a problem when it arises, be it an illness or a conflict in personal relationships. Inconspicuous benefit is good fortune accumulated slowly but steadily, like the growth of a tree or the rising of the tide, which results in the forging of a rich and expansive state of life. We might not discern any change from day to day, but as the years pass, it will be clear that we've become happy, that we've grown as individuals"

The Commissioner fell silent,

"Are you a philosopher as well?" Asked the Commissioner

"I practise the Philosophy of life, I am a Buddhist," replied Roger

"What you've just explained to me is quite profound and makes a lot of sense, you will have to teach me a lot of things," said the Commissioner

"Everyone deserves true happiness," Roger said convincingly, "By the way, was any white and purple coloured handbag retrieved from Charli and his accomplice?"

I have no idea, will certainly check," he replied,

Roger hung up immediately.

On arriving home that afternoon, his parents were out and the house was empty. Suddenly the telephone rang, the person who called said his name was Dick, and wished to speak to Mr Dean.

Since Mr Dean was not available, he said he would call back.

Mr Dean and Marie arrived home late in the evening cold and exhausted they sat in the lounge to watch the TV without bothering to go to their bedroom to change their clothes. Roger was in his room rummaging through his pockets in an attempt to find any note that might bear the clue of where to look for Erika but to no avail. Frustratingly he went into the lounge to watch the TV. Sitting next to his mother, Marie, and listening to their conversation apparently about someone who wished to borrow a large sum of money from Mr Dean. The telephone rang, but Mr Dean and Marie were reluctant to pick it up, so it was ignored and the phone rang off. That prompted Roger to tell Marie that a man whose name was 'Dick' called earlier that day and said he would call back.

"I guess it was him that called a minute ago," said Marie

"I can't get my head round how he lost such a large sums of money twice and not report it, mind boggles," said Mr Dean

Roger's eyes lit up in astonishment in realisation that Dick could be the person who was responsible for the briefcase which he launched at the Victoria station and also the one which was snatched by Charli in the car part near the airport.

There was distinctive silence for a while when suddenly Mr Dean turned round to Roger and asked when he was intending to move out of the family house and get his own place since he did not wish to go back to university and did not wish to find work.

Although, Marie scolded Mr Dean for pressurising Roger to move out but in the deep recesses of her mind she understood that Mr Dean did not feel comfortable with Roger living at home as the two rarely communicated with each other. However, Roger did not utter a word in reply to Mr Dean, he simply and resentfully left the lounge and went back to his room. For two days, Roger did not come out of his room and neither Mr Dean nor Marie attempted to check on him in case it provoked further distasteful consequences.

CHAPTER 19

Jodi, the young man that Julianna met on the train in Monaco while visiting her father at the hospital, the same person who took her to her first Buddhist meeting and introduced her to Buddhism was with Julianna in her penthouse. He had flown in from Monaco to see her.

Julianna and Jodi were getting ready for the monthly Buddhist discussion meeting. A lot of people who attended the basic 'introduction to Buddhism' earlier that month had realised without a doubt the positive transformation the practice of Buddhism had made in their lives, how they had overcome long standing problems and how confident, courageous and compassionate they had become. The most important aspect was the realisation that they were truly happy. In view of these indicators, Julianna was expecting more people than usual at the discussion meeting. She had not seen Soisin since she introduced Erika as her new apartment mate, though when she accidentally met with Erika at Sloane square tube station, she was told by Erika that Soisin had gone to see her uncle Joey in Ireland for a couple of weeks.

Just as she was contemplating calling her because she needed some spare hands to assist with looking after the large number of people she was expecting at the meeting that evening, her telephone rang, for some reason she guessed it would be her,

"Hi Julianna," said Soisin on the phone

"I have been thinking of you," said Julianna

"Me too," she said

"Discussion meeting is today, are you coming?" asked Julianna

"Yes, that's why I rang," she replied

"Great, try and bring your apartment-mate, Erika," requested Julianna

"Will do, see you then," said Soicin

In the evening, Jodi and Julianna had dinner earlier than usual, they expected that perhaps it could be a long meeting so they decided to be quite ready to satisfy members with any questions they might have, no matter how long it took.

It was just before 7.30 pm when some members started drifting in, Jodi decided to lead the chanting of NAM-MYO-HO-RENGE-KYO while they waited for others to arrive before starting the full ceremony which consists of the recitation of the 'Sutra' which means the teaching by the Buddha.

Next to arrive were Soisin and Erika and then the lounge of the penthouse was suddenly full with members. They had settled for the discussion meeting after the primary practice which is the chant and the secondary practice, the recitation of the Sutra. Jodi and Julianna looked around and was pleasantly surprised to realise that most of the people who had attended the 'basics' which was Introduction to Buddhism were all present including some new faces she had not seen before. For that reason, Jodi suggested that everyone should introduce him or herself. Obviously he was ecstatic at the large number of people that were present. Julianna introduced Jodi as the person who introduced her to Buddhism and she encouraged members to ask questions at the end of the meeting, confident that Jodi would be able to answer them. The meeting was vibrant as Jodi resorted to explaining in detail about Benefits of the practice, Buddhahood, world peace, compassion, courage, the fulfilment of one's desires and wisdom.

A few minutes later Roger arrived, as he stood at the entrance he caught sight of Erika sitting beside Soisin, their eyes met and both of them froze with a concoction of ecstasy, delight and monumental astonishment. Their jaws dropped beyond belief. All the people in the room joined in the overwhelming episode that was unfolding, they did not understand why Roger and Erika were in such an irresistible magnetic entrancement.

"Do you know each other?" Asked Julianna

Without much ado, Erika rose from her seat and ran towards Roger who at the same time ran towards Erika, they met almost half way and were gripped in a very tight embrace that lasted for a considerable length of time before extricating themselves from each other. It was unarguably a quintessential part of the entire discussion meeting. Roger therefore, introduced himself and explained to the group that Erika was his lifelong girlfriend and fiancé, but due to some unforeseen circumstance they were separated over a year ago. He also expressed how on his return, he had searched high and low for Erika without success unbeknown to him that they would finally meet in the most unexpected place and circumstance such as here. He glanced at Erika and noticed tears running down her cheeks, she started to sob, gradually at first and then uncontrollably. Julianna rushed into the kitchen and returned with a box of tissue which she handed over to Erika. Roger stopped to explain and assisted in wiping down Erika's tears and pulled her closer to his chest and held her very tightly. That triggered deep emotional feeling from Soisin and some of the members in the group to start weeping for joy. Consequently, the box of tissue was exhausted in an instant and the whole group consumed in silent admiration for the two.

Erika having recovered from her emotive meltdown began to tell her part of the journey. She explained that the reason why she moved out of her apartment was to mandate Roger to look for her because he had been incommunicado for over one year. She added that she was certain that he would search for her and that she was glad her ploy had worked. She also stated that she was searching for him but had no clue where to start and decided to go to Sloane square to look for him because that was the place they had met up and went for a meal earlier.

"So that was why we met at the Sloane square tube last time?" interrupted Julianna

"Yes, I was there every day for a week," answered Erika

"Real love is very powerful indeed," said Jodi

"Great to love and be loved," said Soisin

"Do you know, I have come all the way from Monaco this morning just to see Julianna because I really missed her a lot," said Jodi

This prompted Julianna and most of the people in the group to chuckle, therefore breaking the Ice. To the watchful eyes of the group, Roger knelt down on one knee and asked Erika if she would like to become his wife. Erika's eyes were suddenly filled with joyful tears and she tightly gripped him in an embrace and said yes! Yes! Yes! As they cuddled and kissed several times, the group applauded.

Around 9.00pm the meeting ended by chanting NAM-MYOHO-RENGE-KYO three times. It was inevitable that Erika would not go back to the apartment she shared with Soisin and she was intrinsically sure she would have to follow Roger home that night.

When Roger and Erika finally left, hand in hand of-course, the question that remained unanswered was 'what were the circumstances that led to their separation in the first place.' Jodi, Julianna and Soisin remained in the penthouse after everyone had gone. Julianna mentioned how Roger had not told them what he did or where he lived during the times he had been at the penthouse while Soicin wondered why Erika had not mentioned she had a boyfriend let alone a fiancé. Jodi charismatically added that it was the power of their practice that ensured they were reunited in that solemn circumstance, and he added that the incident was most exhilarating and gratifying.

Mr Dean and Marie were sitting in their lounge watching TV as usual when Roger unexpectedly walked in hand in hand with Erika, they stood face to face with Mr Dean and Marie who were grossly astounded and speechless.

"Mom, Dad, Just to let you know that I and Erika will be getting married soon as I do not wish to let her out of my sight again," Roger announced

"Do you realise you have to get a job first and a house to live in before talking about marriage?" Mr Dean asserted

"Yes, I do," replied Roger

Hand in hand Roger led Erika in to his room.

Marie turned to Mr Dean and said,

"Can't you see that your son has grown up?"

"I don't see it like that, it's more like he has become a child again, how would you expect them to get married without a job and their own place and you call it – growing up?" Asked Mr Dean with sarcasm.

"Give him a chance, will you," replied Marie, "last time you wondered where he got his philosophy from, so let's watch and see what he is capable of,"

"He has not even told us where he had been or what he did for over a year he had been away, and he is now talking about getting married," said Mr Dean

"That is the more reason you should give him a chance," said Marie.

In Roger's room, Roger was cuddled up with Erika earnestly discussing events that transpired since Roger disappeared from his parent's home.

With curiosity Erika asked where he had been and what he did during that time.

He responded that he had been on the train and had no fixed abode and that he had been carrying out what apparently was his mission by providing information which enabled the police department to put criminals behind bars. He expressed his delight in doing that and explained that he had thoroughly enjoyed the experience of living on the trains and the enormous privilege it provided in meeting and intermingling with a variety of characters in the busy world of the train tracks. Erika who was intently listening to his narratives could not comprehend the root causes that led Roger to remove himself from his parents and herself and went to live like a tramp on the trains. However, she had made up her mind to find out the root cause of Roger's sudden strange behaviour which was clearly uncharacteristic of him.

Erika informed Roger that after they had a meal at the 'Rock on' restaurant, the day she went to meet up with him and her hand bag was snatched: she had thought that Roger would return to her or at least kept in touch on a regular basis but unfortunately her dream of reuniting with him became futile. She therefore decided to move out and away from her usual environment in order to curtail and not exacerbate her torture from everything that obviously reminded her of him. At that point Roger asked how she met Soisin, She replied that they had met each other in a supermarket many times before and had said 'hello' to each other until one day she was entering the same super market and saw her picking up her shopping which had littered the entrance floor as a result of a split carrier bag, so, she helped her pick her shopping up. At the end of that, they exchanged telephone numbers and consequently became friends. She added that one day, Soisin telephoned her and asked if she would like to share an apartment with her since the girls who used to be her apartment-mates had moved out and for that reason she required a new apartment-mate. The request from Soisin became an ideal opportunity to leave her apartment and her environment in the knowledge that it would prompt him to search for her and hopefully reunite with her permanently eventually. Roger asked how she met Buddhism and she replied that Soisin introduced her,

"And how did you know about Buddhism," asked Erika

"I met Soisin on the train and she introduced me," replied Roger, "I have been at Julianna's penthouse a couple of times before for Buddhist meeting,

"So, do you believe in destiny?" Asked Erika

"Well, Buddhism calls it karma or the accumulation of Causes and Effects which tend to suggest that one can map out one's destiny or one's path in life, as it says that past causes determine your present circumstances, and the present causes determine future circumstances," replied Roger

"Quite ironical that we were introduce by the same person and we unexpectedly met up at the same place we had attended Buddhist meetings," said Erika with a chuckle

CHAPTER 20

The following morning, both Mr Dean and Marie joined Roger and Erika at the breakfast table which Erika had prepared. The atmosphere at the table was enchanting, Roger was now freely and amicably chatting with his father while Erika seemed to be engaged in conversation with Marie. After the breakfast, Erika washed all the dishes and put them away. Later in the day, Roger and Erika stepped in to the lounge where Mr Dean and Marie were seated, it caused a jaw dropping stare when Roger told them he was going out to look for a job and then he went straight out while Erika stayed back with the intention of having a chat with Marie. Mr Dean also left for his dental appointment. Marie opened a huge cupboard which stood at the far side of the lounge and retrieved a family photo album and re-joined Erika who was pleasantly surprised that the album contained pictures of Roger from his infancy till when he was fifteen years of age. As Marie turned each page, Erika noticed that the 'Train' played very important part in Roger's life. It played out that Roger was conceived on the train which was the Orient Express on his parents' honeymoon, and then during their one year anniversary they also went on the Orient Express and that was when Roger was born, on the Orient Express. Taking a closer look at the toys that Roger had played with since he was a baby, Erika noticed that almost all the toys were to do with Trains. She thought it was certainly bizarre and she wondered if it might have prejudiced Roger's attachment to Trains in his adult hood. Nevertheless, Marie did not notice what could have been the anomaly of purchasing these toys for Roger and Erika did not bring it to her attention.

After they had gone through the album, Erika was ready to leave, she had to go back to her new apartment in the knowledge that Soisin would be anticipating that she would tell her the whole story about her relationship with Roger. She therefore left Marie and went back to her new apartment.

Later in the evening Roger returned home clutching various newspapers including his favourite free evening papers which he had picked up at the train station and immediately started to peruse them on the dining table. Marie asked what he was going to do with them and he replied that jobs were advertised in them. She was chuffed beyond measure that Roger was indeed looking for work as he had promised. He spent a few hours perusing the job section of the newspapers, then finally he took a pen and jotted down some telephone numbers and sat down with Marie to watch TV. As soon as Mr Dean returned from his dental appointment she revealed to him that the newspapers on the dining table were brought in by Roger for job search.

"Did you find anything Roger," asked Mr Dean

"Yes, a couple, I'll call them in the morning for application forms," he replied

"Anything interesting?" enquired Marie

"Just recruitment ad for police officers," he replied

"So you want to join the police force?" asked Mr Dean

"It is a worthwhile job and I intend to give it a go," he replied assuredly

At Erika's new apartment, Soisin had been briefed by Erika about her impending wedding with Roger and how she needed to find a new job to enable them afford a decent apartment of their own. She also informed Soisin that Roger had lived on the train for over one year to which Soisin unexpectedly showed substantial measure of indifference which surprised Erika.

"You do not seem to be overly surprised, Soisin," said Erika

"There are all sorts Erika, especially among gypsy families," said Soisin

"He is not a gypsy," retorted Erika

"I didn't mean he was, In gypsy families we are always careful and choosy about the kind of toys we purchase for children as it could change or influence their lives a great deal," said Soisin

"Did you say 'toys'?" Erika asked

"Yes, especially if the toys reflect the place or circumstances of their birth, it is a strong traditional belief within the gypsy community."

Whether Erika was convinced by the explanation given by Soisin was still left to be seen, nevertheless, the jigsaw definitely fitted accordingly because as Marie had explained to her while showing her the family album: Roger was conceived and was born on the train, he had and played with toy trains which provoked some strange and precarious thought in her mind as to whether or not Roger would eventually go back to live on the train again after their wedding. She could not help but struggled with that conflicting emotions from time to time. However, Soisin told her that she could invite Roger to share their apartment until they got a place of their own, she also informed her that the Arts department Store in the centre of the town had a vacancy for a sales staff. Erika did not spare any time at-all in calling the arts department store and was invited for an interview the following day. Before she could put the phone down Roger called to tell her that he would come over to her apartment that evening to take her to their favourite restaurant. She was delighted and could not wait to tell him the good news of her imminent interview at the Arts department store.

That evening Roger arrived at Erika's apartment and they walked hand in hand to the train station from where they took the train to the 'Rock-on' restaurant. It was not long before they tucked in to the sumptuous meal they ordered. Erika was in fact delirious this time around, due to the fact that she knew they would be leaving together holding hands, unlike the last time they were in the same restaurant and Roger deserted her and went back on the train leaving her to walk home alone, unsure if they would ever meet again.

Roger was pleasantly flabbergasted when told by Erika that she had been invited for a job interview at the Arts department store the following day. He began to envisage the two of them living in an apartment of their own, and eventually some toddlers of their own running around in nappies. However, Roger informed her that he had already made phone calls for an application form for a police officer's vacancy. She noticed from his facial expression that he was so enthused about hopefully becoming a police Officer which became evident when he added that they should be looking for an apartment as soon as possible.

"Why is the hurry," she asked

"Because we need an apartment of our own," She replied

"I should think we need to find work first to enable us to find an apartment," She said

"Soisin had told me some time ago not to look at the problems first but to focus on the goal and then jump each huddle when I came to it," said Roger

"But it is also great wisdom not to run before you can walk," said Erika with a bit of sarcasm.

"It is inappropriate to focus on the difficulties rather than the goal, don't you agree?" asked Roger

Erika did not however agree with him but intentionally decided to keep quiet and say nothing as she noted that arguing with him would certainly not be a good idea because his mind-set had become resolutely fixed.

Two weeks' later, Erika was notified she was successful at the interview, so she started her new job almost immediately. Meanwhile, Roger's application was not successful but he was not deterred. He phoned up for another application form which he filled in confidently but without haste, on completion, he signed 'Eyeball' for his name, dated it and sent off. When this application reached the Police department's Human Resources department, it caused some stir when they came across his signature 'Eyeball'. The form was hastily rushed on to the Commissioner, Colin Smith.

Roger had gone to the Arts department store where Erika worked to escort her home as it was his usual practice to accompany her to work and to escort her back home to the apartment when she had finished her shift in the evenings. Mr Dean and Marie were in their home when unexpectedly there was a knock at the front door, peering through the window they could see a police car with two police escorts on police motorbikes. Mr Dean and Marie gazed at each other in silent wonder, Mr Dean opened the front door and was overwhelmed to see that it was indeed the Commissioner of police standing at their front door. Mr Dean knew too well that he was the Commissioner because he had come to see him some time before when he was just a Detective Inspector Colin Smith, who was assigned to investigate the Victoria station incident. However, this time around he was kitted in a highly respectful and ceremonial corporate outfit, he had seen him many times on TV, and his pictures were frequently in Newspapers. The Commissioner checked again the address on the application form in his hand which was submitted by Roger, having confirmed he was at the correct address, he introduced himself and asked if he could come in. Mr Dean still dazed held the door wide open and invited him in.

"I believe we had met before," said the Commissioner

"Certainly, but you were different then," replied Mr Dean

"I am the same person, just in a different uniform," he said, "I will like to speak to your son,"

"I am afraid he is not here right now," replied Mr Dean

At that very moment the front door opened and Roger rushed in with Erika following behind. They had seen the police car and the motorbikes in front of the house and became curious,

"Eyeball?" Asked the Commissioner

"Yes," replied Roger

"I am not here to arrest you, would you like to come with me to the police headquarters?"

"I will take my fiancé over to her apartment first and then go over to the police headquarters," said Roger

"You do not seem to understand, you have to come with me now," said the Commissioner

Roger was immediately escorted to the police car by the two escorts with little resistance, although Erika insisted on going with them but she was not allowed. When Roger was whisked to the police headquarters he had no idea what would be the outcome, at the same time Mr Dean thought they might not see him again for a very long time while Marie passed out and was rushed to the hospital.

CHAPTER 21

At the Police headquarters, Roger was dumbfounded to find he was in the office of the Commissioner instead of the cell block. Both he and the commissioner were in this office for several hours with the door shut. After intensive private conversation, Roger was escorted home by the same escorts who had earlier brought him in, this time the Commissioner stayed back in his office.

When Roger got home there was no-one in the house, neither Mr Dean nor Marie was at home. So he called Erika who informed him that his mother Marie, passed out when he was taken away and consequently was rushed to the hospital. However, Erika was pleased to hear from Roger but she still had reservations whether he had finally been released. She did not want to ask Roger immediately because she knew for a fact that Roger's priority was his dear mother's well-being. Roger immediately went to the hospital and found his father at her bed side. She was very poorly. His father was relieved because he did not expect to see him again, at least not soon. His mother was still unconscious and unaware that Roger had arrived. Few minutes later, the consultant came in on his round to attend to her. It was during this time that she opened her eyes slightly and saw Roger standing at her bedside with his father,

"Mother, it's me Roger, I am back," whispered Roger

His mother suddenly sat up, gazed at Roger for a few seconds and then stared into nothingness in disbelief, she tilted her head toward him, held his hand and squeezed it gently and held on to it.

Marie's hospitalization was short-lived, her speedy recovery was due to the fact that her only son whom she had thought she might not see again in the foreseeable future had suddenly and unexpectedly appeared at her bedside - the same day that he was taken away. That evidently restored her faith in humanity.

The following morning she was discharged from the hospital, to add to her contentment it was Roger, Erika and Mr Dean that took her home together.

In the evening of that day, they were watching TV after dinner when Mr Dean turned to Roger and asked,

"Why were you taken away yesterday?" asked Mr Dean

"I have no idea," replied Roger

"Very unusual to be arrested by the Commissioner himself," said Erika.

"Did they not give you any reason for picking you up?" asked Mr Dean

"Not a clue, Dad," replied Roger

Marie was simply passing glances as they spoke, she did not say anything, she was simply satisfied that her son was back.

Erika went to the kitchen and moments later emerged with a pot of tea and some biscuits which she served and took her seat again.

Roger told them that the full intentions of the police for picking him up would be made known to him at his next meeting with the Commissioner,

"Meeting with the Commissioner? You've gone up in the world," said Mr Dean

"They are not going to pick you up again, are they?" asked Marie curiously

"No mom, I will simply meet up with him in his office," Roger replied.

"I believe you have not disclosed anything to us, you are hiding something, the commissioner of police does not go round houses picking people up with his escorts," Mr Dean said with cynicism

"It is a long story Dad, it will all be revealed at my next meeting with him.

CHAPTER 22

The Commissioner Colin Smith had just returned from one of the many meetings with the Home Office minister, sitting in his office reminiscing of how he had not only saved his career but also gained promotions for solving many extraordinary criminal cases. He could not have achieved all these without the help of Roger, alias 'Eyeball.' Deep down in the dark recesses of his being he realised he owed him a lot but could not comprehend how to show his gratitude. However, he had managed to conceal his true feelings to Roger, alias 'Eyeball.'

He knew that the arrest of Charli and her accomplice in connection with the briefcase was still open ended because the owner of the brief case was still at large and had not reported the loss of the briefcase to the police, and for that reason it set off alarm bells.

The next challenge was the Victoria station incident. He knew that Roger was responsible for hurling the briefcase at the transport police team standing at the ticket barrier because he was caught on camera. The question was 'how and where he got hold of the briefcase.' Again no-one had reported it missing. In contemplation, he had decided to put these concerning questions to Roger when they meet again. It was not rocket science to understand that where-ever these briefcases came from, that the owners had criminal implications otherwise they would have been reported to the police.

There was a knock at his office door,

"Come in," said the Commissioner

It was a jaw dropping scenario when Charlee, the real fiancé of the commissioner was led in by two escorts. He was frozen and overawed with disbelief that for a couple of minutes he was totally speechless as he and Charlee fixed stern glances at each other. The two escorts were equally bewildered and simply closed the door behind them as they left the office. Unexpectedly to the Commissioner, Charlee was furious and asked him why he was not taking her calls.

It played out that Charlee who was engaged to be married to the Commissioner had an identical twin sister, too identical that even their parents had difficulty in identifying them, to add to the confusion, the two identical twins had similar names. Charlee was the commissioner's fiancée and her identical delinquent twin sister was called Charli. He was aware his fiancée Charlee, had a twin sister but they had never met and Charlee did not wish to introduce her twin sister because of the strange path she had chosen.

Charlee had gone to France to visit her God-son and was arrested in front of Nice railway station allegedly for snatching hand bags and she had been locked up since then. Eventually she was allowed to make a phone call, so, she rang her fiancé, the Commissioner several times but could not reach him.

What actually happened was that prior to her arrival in Nice, her twin sister Charli had snatched a few hand bags in Nice France, and was caught on camera, however, she successfully escaped with her loot and returned to the UK while the French police was still looking for her. Consequently, on Charlee's arrival in Nice she was apprehended by the police as the handbag snatcher, obviously mistaken for the real culprit due to their stunning resemblance. Unfortunately she had been unable to convince the police she was the wrong person until the Interpol confirmed that another lady who fitted that description was in the hands of the British police for snatching handbags in London. It was also confirmed that the lady's name was Charli and had left France a couple of days before Charlee was arrested. As a result, Charli was allowed to leave without charge.

After listening to her story, the Commissioner, stood up from her seat and led her to the cell where her twin sister Charli was locked up, for verification. Inside the cell Charli was sitting down on the floor when her cell door was opened and her sister Charlee and the Commissioner entered. Both sisters were standing face to face staring at each other in silent rebuke. He noticed that their striking resemblance was unarguably astounding, so, he led Charlee by the hand and they walked back to the office. He explained to her that after her sister was arrested, he was disappointed because he thought it was her. Because of that, he deleted her number and blocked it with the intention that she would not reach him again. He apologised for failing to contact her. After the dust seemed to have settled.

"You have gone up in the world, what happened?" asked Charlee

"Yes, I have been promoted, I am now the Commissioner," he replied

"It was not very long ago that you were threatened with losing your job, and look at where you are now, It is a miracle," said Charlee

"Do you know what that means?" asked the Commissioner

"What is it supposed to mean?" asked Charlee

"It means that our wedding is back on track," replied the Commissioner

The Commissioner impulsively got down on one knee and proposed marriage to her only to be disappointed that her answer was not in the affirmative. He got up, though deflated but undeterred, he left the office and took Charlee to lunch.

CHAPTER 23

Ten days later, Roger was on his way to the Commissioner's office for a meeting which was scheduled in the afternoon of that day. He took the train from his local train station. Sitting in one of the carriages, he was in reminiscent of the days gone-by when he was some sort of a super tramp aimlessly gallivanting from station to station without any particular destination. Deep down, he cherished all the antics and shenanigans that were always taking place within the grand theatre of the train carriages by total strangers, a stage in which it was free for all to perform, irrespective of talent. It was a natural mandate by which a song which was in every-one's heart filtered out and inevitably escaped uncontrollably like the smoke from the tiniest of seams.

He treasured all his experiences on the train, nevertheless, his focus at that moment was about the meeting he was about to have with the Commissioner in less than an hour. He reflected on his past communications with him and wondered if he remembered he was responsible for the Victoria station's incident and he decided to come clean even if he was not questioned about that. He also was determined to mention to him about Dick, the man who called his father on telephone. Since Marie had said something to Mr Dean about Dick having lost a large sum of money twice and not reported it, it was therefore imperative for Dick to be investigated.

Few minutes later, his train pulled up at the station quite close to the police headquarter where Roger alighted. He showed the pass which was given to him previously at the security desk and was let in. The commissioner was already waiting when Roger entered his office. Again he shut the office door and instructed his Personal Assistant to hold all calls. For several hours they remained in the office, just two of them. They had discussed among other things, Roger's aspirations and his intention to become a police officer and then finally,

"Can you tell me about the briefcase at the Victoria station?" he asked

"Sure, I found it on the train, the lady in whose possession it was, was sitting opposite me on the train and when the train stopped at a station, two police officers casually entered the train, the lady left abruptly and hurriedly leaving the briefcase on his seat, so I picked it up with the intention of handing it over to the police so they could trace the lady and reunite her with it," said Roger

"Were the two police officers looking for her?" asked the Commissioner

"I do not think so, they entered the train and walked through the adjoining doors to the other carriage, thinking about it now, perhaps she had thought the two officers were after her, therefore, she panicked and left the train very quickly leaving the briefcase on the seat," Roger replied

"Did you know what was inside?" He asked

"I had no idea," replied Roger

"Why did you hurl it at the group of transport police at the exit barrier?" he asked

"Because I had no valid ticket so I had to run," Replied Roger

"If you knew it contained over three hundred thousand pounds would you have kept it," he asked

"No, perhaps I might be rewarded for handing it in," Roger replied, "but that's not the point,"

The Commissioner fell silent.

There is a mystery surrounding the briefcase, real mystery indeed," he said with a groan,

"What is the mystery?" Roger asked

"The briefcase has not been claimed and neither was it reported missing," he added, "and that also goes for the other briefcase which was snatched at the car park near the airport,"

"If that was the case, it seems to me that the same person was responsible for both briefcases, but the question still remains, 'why they were not reported stolen or missing,'" said Roger

"My team is on the trail of the two men and the woman in the car park, one of the men was called Err... Dee,"

"It could also mean 'Dick'," Roger intervened

"Yes, he is particularly interesting to us," he said, "and I dare say young man, you have a sharp mind of an excellent detective,"

"Thank you, Boss," said Roger

At the end of a heart to heart exchange, both could perceive some significant degree of trust in each other, they shook hands.

Roger was about to leave the office when he called him back and handed over to him a large document wallet containing a pack of documents and other accessories,

"I have discussed with the home office minister about you, and he agreed to my request, it's all in this pack, study it carefully sign what you need to sign and return the documents to me accordingly." he advised.

Roger delightfully accepted the document wallet and about to leave again, the Commissioner called him back and said,

"Do not forget, you've to teach me your splendid philosophy,"

Roger's face joyfully lit up,

"I am at your service anytime, I will bring some books for you to read and get acquainted with the teachings of the Buddha," Replied Roger, "but in the meantime, chant NAM-MYO-HO-RENGE-KYO whenever you can and as often as you can,"

He gave him a card which explains the one essential phrase.

"When we manifest the life of this phrase in ourselves, we will be able to make everything in the universe function for our benefit." Roger added

"Thank you, detective inspector 'Eyeball' or shall I say - Roger Dean?" he asked

Roger was momentarily taken aback when the commissioner addressed him as detective Inspector.

"Thank you, boss," replied Roger

"Your journey is truly incandescent of the proof of your philosophy," he said

CHAPTER 24

Mr Dean, Marie and Erika were sitting in the lounge at home waiting to hear the news about Roger's meeting with the Commissioner. They had been sitting for an interminable period of six hours and began to wonder if he had been placed in police custody. The fact that Roger had not told them anything regarding the frequent police visits at their house and subsequently by the Commissioner conjured ominous reservations. However, they gritted their teeth and hopped for the best.

Meanwhile, Roger was on a home-bound train reminiscing his long meeting with the Commissioner and at the same time curious about what was contained in the document wallet which he was in deed looking forward to finding out. Suddenly, a busker playing a wind instrument - the harmonica, entered the carriage through the adjoining doors in which Roger was sitting and began to play soothing and melodic tunes in anticipation that passengers would throw some money in the hat he displayed between his feet. Though the passengers seemed to be enjoying the music because they stole glances with a smile but none threw any money in the hat. Roger was farther away in the carriage listening to the pleasant and eclectic tunes the busker was producing. The busker then stopped and began to move on farther along the carriage. Just then, a woman who looked like she was imbued with a touch of eccentricity screamed on top of her voice,

"More! More! More!"

She continued with the scream until the passengers joined in.

The busker by now was standing not far from where Roger was sitting, and commenced his performance again with much vigour. The satisfaction that he felt as the passengers screamed for more was easily discernible in his face. The acentric woman got up, unzipped her enormous hand bag, took out a violin and jammed with the busker in an impromptu musical jamboree. It was not long before the busker's hat was filled with coins and paper money. The eccentric woman left her violin case open on the floor which was also instantly filled with money.

Roger quietly rummaged through his pocket and put a twenty pound note into the hat which was already overflowing with money, and then he felt a slight tap on his shoulder. He turned round and it was the detective Sergeant Jake sitting right behind him,

"If you keep giving out twenty pound notes you'll soon be skint," said detective sergeant jokingly,

"Why do you keep following me - tramp?" Asked Roger jokingly

"I could ask the same about you," he replied

"Where are you off to this time?" asked Roger

"Working to find someone to nick," he replied

'nick' is a slang for arrest.

"How come the boss is singing your praises?" asked Sergeant Jake, "It's left the entire headquarters bewildered,"

"Who is the boss that you are talking about," Roger asked

"The police commissioner," replied Sergeant Jake

"If that was the case, I have no idea," Roger replied

Roger was enthused to find out more about Sergeant Jake and his utterances but he had reached his final station and he could not wait to go home and find out what was in the document wallet, he thought perhaps that the mystery document wallet contained most of the answers to the questions that kept flooding his mind such as when the Commissioner called him 'detective Inspector Eyeball.'

CHAPTER 25

Roger got home and opened the front door, he went in to find his mother, father and Erika sitting in the lounge anticipating to hear about his meeting with the Commissioner.

However, contrary to their expectation that Roger would sit down with them to tell them what had transpired with regard to his meeting with the Commissioner, Roger walked past the lounge without saying a word to them, went into his room and locked himself in. His attitude fuelled their conviction that perhaps his meeting with the Commissioner was indeed negative and therefore that Roger was in a lot of trouble. Though very anxious, they considered it would be better to leave him alone until he was ready to discuss.

Roger remained in his room going through the documents in the wallet one by one and signed what required his signature. It also contained a set of keys for a large apartment, a job offer for the post of detective inspector. After going through the contents of the wallet, Roger was awe-struck and wondering how all his wishes had come true unexpectedly. He laid down in bed staring at a blank wall consumed in joyful ecstasy, then he fell asleep.

The following morning while they were all having breakfast Marie asked,

"How is the job hunting going, Roger?

"I am not job-hunting anymore, I have got a job," replied Roger convincingly

"That was a sudden change of mind, so you no longer wish to be a police office?" Mr Dean asked.

"You are now speaking to a detective Inspector Roger Dean, Dad," he said, "and I will be moving into my new apartment in two weeks' time,"

"So you have a job and an apartment," enquired Erika

"That's correct," replied Roger calmly

"If that is the case, then I'll believe in miracle," said Mr Dean

There were no further questions instead there was complete silence, each wondering what did transpire for Roger to deserve all that. After the breakfast Roger quickly put the documents that he had signed in an envelope kissed Erika and left the house.

Marie said to Mr Dean,

"Did I not tell you he had grown up?"

Mr Dean did not reply but fixed his gaze at a blank wall with permanent smile on his face and so did Erika.

Two weeks later

Roger moved into his new apartment with Erika. It was a majestic and an imposing apartment situated by the banks of the river Thames not far from Julianna's penthouse. He stood on the balcony admiring the striking views across the river and the bridge, it had the same magical effect on him just as it did the first time he stood on Juliana's penthouse balcony. Erika was busy in the kitchen preparing sumptuous dinner. The apartment was fully furnished and in excellent condition. Erika laid the dinner on the dining table, poured out two glasses of wine and joined Roger on the balcony. As she handed a glass of wine to him, she said:

"It happened so fast, Roger,"

"I still cannot believe this is happening to us," said Roger

"When will you start your job?" asked Erika

"In two weeks' time," replied Roger

Roger contacted Juliana and told her that he would like to host the next Buddhist meeting at his new apartment to which she delightfully accepted. Roger did not waste any time in inviting his parents and the Commissioner to the meeting.

On the following Sunday evening Buddhist members and guests began to converge at Roger and Erika's new address. Julianna, Jodi and Soisin were the first to arrive followed by the commissioner who was wearing a simple jeans trousers and T shirt.

Roger took him aside to the balcony and expressed his appreciation for believing in him and for making his wishes come true. The commissioner reciprocated by expressing his gratitude to Roger for enabling him to save his career and subsequently gaining rapid promotion,

"This is actual proof of the power which the price of a sandwich and coffee at the station's platform could have," said the commissioner,

"In Buddhism it is called the actual proof of the power of practice." Said Roger

As both of them reverberated into thunderous laughter, he put his hands on Roger's shoulder and they walked back into the lounge where he introduced the commissioner to Erika, Julianna, Jodi and Soisin. Few minutes' later, Roger's parents Marie and Mr Dean arrived followed by the rest of the Buddhist members and guests.

The Buddhist discussion meeting started and ended with the usual exuberance joy. The Commissioner was the first to ask for books or magazines that would assist him to know more about the practice.

CHAPTER 26

The Inspector's first day in the office

Roger entered his office as the Detective Inspector. It was a spacious office and fully furnished with all mod-cons. He sat on a leathery revolving chair behind a huge desk with drawers and two telephones. One of the phones rang, he picked it up a voice came through, clear and loud,

"Is that detective Inspector Roger Dean?

"Yes, who is speaking?" asked the Inspector

"It's the commissioner, I hope you are settling in fine," said the commissioner

"Very well, thank you," acknowledged the Inspector

"Your team will be introducing themselves to you, Sergeant Jake will be attending to any immediate concerns you may have and I will be sending my deputy to support you until you settle in properly," the commissioner assured him.

"Thank you, Boss," replied the Inspector

Shortly after his conversation with the commissioner there was a knock at the door. Sergeant Jake entered with a colleague to introduce themselves as some of the members of his team. The Inspector

MIKE IKE CHINWUBA

shook their hands and said to Sergeant Jake that he did not require introduction since they had met many times before,

"Thank you, boss – good to see you," said Sergeant Jake, "I knew it, you were not just a student writing thesis about trains,"

"Remember, there is no school on the train," said the Inspector

Sergeant Jake and the Inspector erupted with laughter, the Sergeant and his colleague left the office.

Outside the office Sergeant Jake's colleague said with resentment,

"He is just a boy, what experience has he got to be the boss,"

"Do not judge a book by its cover, I have seen him at work, he is the shadow of the shadows – believe me," said Sergeant Jake.

In the afternoon of the same day The Inspector left his office and went to the train station about to board a train when he came face to face with Sergeant Jake on the platform. The Sergeant was astonished and asked the Inspector.

"How come you are here doing my job, boss?

"I am not cut out to sit in the office chair languishing, I need to be on the trains to be proactive, that's where I am most effective – so, here I am again."

The detective Inspector Roger Dean alias 'Eyeball' slowly turned round and confidently entered the train.

Lightning Source UK Ltd.
Milton Keynes UK
UKOW04f0612280216

269196UK00001B/56/P